WHERE IN THE WORLD

A 'THE ONE FOR US' UNIVERSE STANDALONE

TL HAMILTON

TL HAMILTON

Where in the World

Copyright © 2022 by TL Hamilton

Cover Art © Kismet New Moon Designs 2022

Editing: Kaye Kemp Editing Services

Proofreading: Heart Full of Reads

10 9 8 7 6 5 4 3 2 1

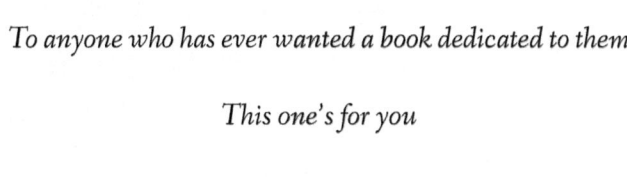

To anyone who has ever wanted a book dedicated to them

This one's for you

CHAPTER ONE

Rowen

"Ok, guys, that's all from me for now. Until next time, remember, you only live once, so live chic!"

I signed off from my vlog with a sigh of relief. Finally, the series was finished. Fashion wasn't my ideal choice of content, but when I did a controversial or serious series, I needed to balance it with the fluff to keep viewers, sponsors, and my mother happy. Not an easy feat. Especially when my mother was a traditionalist when it came to women: control from the background, spend as much as your husband—because you had to have a husband—-earns, and only engage in womanly pursuits. Her standards were stifling, and I frequently failed in every single area of expectation.

My lifestyle vlog had recently hit nine hundred thousand followers, and as much as I wanted to create content that mattered, becoming financially independent was my top priority.

Pushing up from the desk, I switched off the circle light and removed my phone from its stand, mentally packing thoughts of my parents away while I physically stowed my equipment.

The plush shag carpet tickled my bare feet as I crossed my sparse bedroom to the walk-in wardrobe, stripping out of the extremely uncomfortable, yet fashionable, clothing items I'd been reviewing as I went.

If I were honest, my apartment was far too large for one person, but I had appearances to maintain, and the spacious penthouse was enough to keep my mother out of my hair. The fact I kept it almost empty was my own private rebellion. As was my choice of friends.

Pulling a pair of yoga pants up over my hips, I put my phone on speaker and hit up my besties to celebrate.

Makenna picked up on the fifth ring, as always.

"I think I heard the beginning of a sixth ring there. Are the boys trying to throw off your groove?" I asked.

Makenna lived in a shared house with four guys. Dream or nightmare, it was hard to tell, but I often joked she could have her own harem if she stopped acting like one of the guys.

A snort came down the line in response to my teasing.

"There is never a sixth ring, and you know it. What's going on?"

I smirked at my friend's obsession with the number five and shrugged into an oversized sweater, slicking my hair into a short ponytail as I spoke. "Just finished the fashion review series, so it's time to celebrate. Turn off your computer and come hang with me."

Mak grunted, and through the phone came the unmistakable tap of her keyboard. I waited for her to finish whatever line of code she was writing before bringing her back to the conversation.

"I have a family-size bag of Hershey's kisses..."

I let the offer hang in the air. Less than a minute later, the chime of her computer shutting down brought a grin to my face.

"Sloane is here watching *Shifting Sands* again. I'll drag her into the Uber as soon as the commercials start."

I didn't bother arguing. *Shifting Sands* was an over-acted, ridiculously dramatized television program most of us had grown out of watching when we were in our teens. Not Sloane, though. Superfan would be an understatement.

We had all seen every episode to date and knew every detail of Thane's story, and his ongoing dispute with the supervillain, Draven. Personally, I thought Draven was a much more interesting character than Thane, but saying so in front of Sloane wasn't worth the drama. She'd had enough shit in her life, and if a fictional man made her happy? I wasn't messing with it.

I promised the television would be ready for her when they arrived and hung up with a chuckle as the shouting started. Clearly, Makenna's need for candy took precedence over

Shifting Sands. My girls had their quirks, but they were the best friends I could ever hope to have.

The clothing from earlier went into a hamper, and I took a moment to put away the things I had used throughout the day. I hated clutter, possibly a pushback against the excess I grew up with, and frequently donated large portions of my belongings to charity. Did it mean I occasionally found I no longer owned things I needed? Yes, but I had the means to replace them. There were so many people out there who couldn't do it as easily as I could. My wanderings took me into the kitchen, where I stopped dead at the sight of a large bouquet of blood-red roses sitting in the middle of my breakfast table. Where the hell had they come from?

I hated all cut flowers—why kill them just so they can rot on your table—but roses were the worst. The floral embodiment of cliche, the stupid flower that supposedly symbolized love, was boring and didn't even smell good. I would've suspected Makenna left them as a prank, except that she had an even lower opinion of love and all its trappings than I did. One of the guys, perhaps. Makenna's roommates liked to mess with her, and us by extension. They had a way of knowing exactly how to get under her skin.

In case Wolf had found a way to break in and prank me, I left the flowers untouched and flopped onto my lounge suite to wait for my girls. Grabbing my tablet from the coffee table, I scrolled through socials and responded to the latest comments on my vlog before switching to my emails with a sigh.

A loud ping signaled a new email, the sender line making me sit forward in my seat, brow creased, as I clicked it open.

From: FBI<jacko18392@gmail.com>

To: Me

Hello.

You r in our records for tax evasion. If you do not transfer $650,000USD to our offises within 24 hours you will be killed. Click this link to transfer funds.

If you have questions, cal this number +34 571 74 53 01

Regards

FBI

I straightened, reading and re-reading the correspondence that had so rudely invaded my inbox. I wasn't sure if I was more concerned that someone had threatened to kill me, or offended that my life was only worth $650k. Rude. I was sure I should be worth at least three times that.

I sighed, sitting back in my chaise lounge, and let my tablet rest in my lap while I contemplated my options. The email was clearly not from the FBI—I wasn't an idiot—but normal scammers would threaten to arrest me. These guys expressly said kill, and while they clearly couldn't spell "offices", I didn't want to see how easily they could track me down.

They had emailed my private account. That was a concern. No one had access to my private email. After my vlog series on hackers went viral, I had been far more careful to keep my public influencer side separate from my private life.

The intercom beside my door buzzed, announcing Makenna and Sloane's arrival. Damn, I should have asked them to bring pizza.

Email forgotten, I jogged to the speaker to ask the doorman to let them up. I had tried repeatedly to give blanket approval for the girls to be allowed into the building, but after the elderly gentleman at the front of my building almost had a heart attack over the break of protocol, I had to accept it wasn't going to happen.

"Let them up," I called into the intercom, then hesitated for a moment. "Hey, Steve, did you bring flowers up to my apartment today?"

There was a moment where I could almost feel his desire to tell me to go fuck myself. He'd never let me win like that, though. Protocol stated that the doorman announced visitors who, of course, had their identity confirmed, and the resident would then accept or decline the visitation. I'd also been reminded on several occasions that his name was Stephen. Nicknames were considered crass in the circles my family moved in.

Listening closely, I heard the small gust of a sigh before he replied in a voice that was as composed as ever. "I was led to believe madam didn't care for flowers. If they had been delivered here, I would have returned them immediately, as per your instructions."

Right. So clearly, it was one of Makenna's housemates screwing with me.

A chiming in the hallway a moment later announced the elevator car's arrival, and my friends with it. I threw my door open to greet them and stepped back immediately to avoid Sloane who barreled through the door en route to the television and flicked it on to *Shifting Sands*. Makenna shrugged, giving me a one-armed hug around the laptop bag she had slung over her shoulder, and headed to the kitchen.

"Hi, guys," I said, standing alone in the foyer as my friends made themselves at home.

"Rowen," Mak called from the kitchen.

"Cupboard on the left."

"Got it."

She reappeared a moment later, shedding pieces of foil as she inhaled the bag of Hershey's Kisses I always kept on hand for her visits.

"Hey, where'd those flowers come from?" she asked.

"Very funny. You can take them back with you when you go. Has Wolf worked out how to break in here? I'll have to grill him on how he got past Steve."

"No one can get past Steve."

Makenna watched me closely for a minute before turning back toward the kitchen.

"It wasn't Wolf. He's been away all week. When did they turn up?"

I followed her through the apartment and watched as she retrieved a white card from the middle of the arrangement.

"I dunno. Sometime this afternoon, I think. Steve said he didn't bring anything up. Could it have been one of the other guys?"

Mak frowned at the card and flipped it toward me.

"What happens in twenty-four hours?" she asked.

This wasn't funny. It also definitely, probably, wasn't a prank from one of the guys.

"Someone's going to kill me."

CHAPTER TWO

Rowen

"HANG ON A MINUTE, WHY NOT JUST PAY THE MONEY out?" Makenna asked, far too reasonably, as I threw clothes at the sports bag I'd left in the center of my bed.

"Aside from the fact that it was an insulting amount, they've proven they can get to me. The thing about blackmail is if you pay it once, there's nothing stopping them from doing it again."

What I didn't mention was that my parents had drilled into me from a young age that, if I was ever kidnapped and held to ransom, they would not be handing over a dime. It was my responsibility to keep myself safe.

That's right. I was born into a family that had abduction procedures. If I could legally file for emancipation at twenty-five years old and avoid an increase in the frequency of my mother's phone calls telling me what an embarrassment I was to the family name, I would have done so. Unfortunately, any public sign that we were less than the perfect family would be met with the harshest of consequences. Even as an adult, I was stuck.

I felt genuinely irritated at the small amount these scammers were asking—I was worth far more than that, thank you—and had come up with a brilliant plan somewhere between trashing the goddamn roses and choosing an outfit I could fly in comfortably.

"If they want to kill me, they'll have to find me first. I'll fly all over the world, do a vlog series, and give hints about my location. I'll move on every twenty-four hours to stay safe, and my followers will love it. Win-win."

"That doesn't sound like the best idea," Sloane said, resting her shoulder on my doorframe.

An advertisement for Jell-O blasted in the background, proving it wasn't the drama unfolding in my apartment that had pulled her away from her show. Just an ad break.

"What if they catch up to you? You're going to be all alone."

"I'm always alone," I muttered, tossing a pair of sandals on top of my bathing suit.

Sloane was across the room in two steps, wrapping me in a hug. She gave the biggest, warmest hugs in the world, despite being the smallest of us all.

"You've always got us. You know that," she whispered.

"Yeah, I do. Sorry," I said, backing reluctantly out of her arms to continue packing.

"I really think you should let me investigate these people. Give me a few hours to see who they are," Mak said, tossing another candy into her mouth as Sloane drifted back toward the television.

"I'm not letting you hack the hackers. Let me have my adventure and don't get yourself killed trying to help," I insisted. After a moment, I added, "Though if you could hack the airline and delay my flight by thirty minutes, I'll love you forever."

Makenna rolled her eyes and went to retrieve her laptop as the intercom buzzed.

"Uber's here," I announced unnecessarily.

Sloane shushed me, attention fixed to the screen as a gaunt-faced woman swooned in Thane's strong embrace. Or some shit like that.

"Sloane, stop drooling over Hottie McHotface. Get over here and wish me luck with my not dying."

"You're not going to die," she insisted again.

"I might. Poor little rich girl like me. My plane could go down. I could get mixed up with a dangerous crowd. These bad guys could actually be bad and legit kill me."

Sloane snorted and peeled herself off the couch to kiss my cheek while herding me out the door. "None of the above is going to happen. You'll traipse all over the world until you get bored, probably have a whirlwind romance or two, then come home and let us both live vicariously through you. I love you. Now go, so Mak doesn't have to commit any more federal crimes to fix your timetable."

I chuckled, blew a kiss to my besties, and headed down to my waiting Uber.

***

"... so, bestie babes, follow my journey, figure out the clues about where I am, and let's see if we're smarter than these scammers. This is episode one of my new vlog series, 'Where in The World'. Remember, you only live once, so live chic!"

A heavy blow landed on my calf as I signed off, followed by a shrieking cry.

I stumbled, then turned to see a harried-looking woman balancing a crying baby on one hip and screaming after two blonde heads that disappeared under the feet of the crowd as she erratically waved a suitcase that I was sure had issued the blunt force trauma to my lower leg.

"You had to travel cattle class," I muttered as I weaved through the masses to find my departure gate.

Last call piped almost incoherently through the overhead speakers, and I broke into a jog, using elbows where necessary to make sure I was on my flight.

I shouldn't have stopped to film my intro post, I knew that, but I couldn't pass up the aesthetic of the terminal. Where would I go? What came next? It was such a transitory backdrop. I loved it. The double doors were half-closed as I hit the departure lounge at a run, throwing myself toward the ticket desk.

"Wait!"

Two perfectly dressed women froze, and from the corner of my eye, I saw a huge-ass security guard stir, as though wondering if this crazy screaming lady was going to give them any trouble.

"Are you Rowen Black?" one woman asked, subtly waving off the big guy.

"Yes! Yes, that's me. Can I please get on?"

"You were paged three times. Your flight is about to leave."

Shit. They could have called me, but the sound quality was so poor I honestly hadn't bothered to listen. I flexed my hands, trying to think of a plan to talk myself onto the flight, when the second woman gasped.

"Oh, shit! Rowen! Dee, this is Rowen! As in Living Chic. She's amazeballs! I just got a notification you had a new post up. I was waiting for my break to watch it. New series? I'm here for it!"

There was so much enthusiasm oozing from the poor girl, it took me a moment of stunned disbelief to realize I may have found my ticket to ride... so to speak. I already felt dirty. The number of times I'd seen my parents do a similar thing to get their way was horrible, but money and fame talked, and I needed to be on that flight.

Pasting on what I hoped was a winning smile, I focused on her, gripping her shoulder tightly.

"Okay, so total exclusive, my next series is a travel theme. I need on that flight to get my content. Can you help a girl out? You would literally be saving my life here." I didn't want to think about the possibility there could be truth to the statement, so I just smiled wider, agreed to a thousand selfies, and finally, I was walking through the jetway to the airplane.

A slow, totally sarcastic clap started as I tripped and half skipped my way down the aisle to my seat. Matching their energy, I stopped to take a bow before continuing my progress.

Perhaps stupidly, I had kept my bag as carry-on, and now, being so late, I had the extra stress of finding where to stow the stupid thing. All the overhead room was taken up around my seat, and just as I was about to give up, a really tall body stepped into the aisle with me, grabbed my bag, and shoved it into a spot I could have sworn wasn't there a moment before.

"Sit down, so we can go," he grunted, before sliding into his seat. The aisle seat. Next to my window seat.

I grimaced and tried to edge by him. He did that polite thing where you kind of half lift up to get your knees out of the way.

Ass or tits? Ass or tits? I never knew which way to choose when I had to get past someone in close quarters. It was always a dilemma. Tits, I decided. Somehow, I couldn't see this guy appreciating my ass in his face while I squeezed through to my seat.

I got my left foot past relatively drama-free and was ready to breathe a sigh of relief when my right foot caught and I fell chest first into his face. Shit. I pulled back just enough to see the guy. His pink lips pursed in a way that I shouldn't have found sexy. Especially when I didn't know him. Especially, especially when...

"Is there a reason you're straddling me?"

I laughed nervously. "Well, I was trying to avoid kneeing you in the balls. It seemed polite, seeing as we haven't met yet. Although, we should at least be friends now, what with how well you've recently gotten to know my boobs. They have names, you know?" *Oh my God, Rowen, shut up!*

As my mouth continued to run away from me, the guy did the single hottest thing he could have. With no evidence of effort, he lifted me entirely off his lap and placed me carefully in the seat next to him. Then reached across my lap and buckled me in.

"We're good to go. Let's get this bird in the air," he called to the steward closest to us, then settled back in his seat, eyes resolutely to the front.

"How long is this flight?" I wondered out loud as the flight attendant at the front of the plane rattled off the safety precautions.

A long sigh came from the guy next to me as he brushed his hand back and forth over his short, wheat-colored hair. Really short, now that I looked at it. Maybe he was in the military. I considered thanking him for his service, but the chances of his mood improving with the thanks weren't worth the risk if I got it wrong. I didn't want to make him more pissy than he already was.

"About eleven hours. You didn't know that already?"

I hadn't. It wasn't like I'd put a whole lot of thought into this plan. I was just kinda winging it.

Faced with an eleven-hour flight, it occurred to me I was going to need a better thought-out itinerary if I didn't want to spend all my time crushed into tiny seats, eating stale bags of peanuts.

At least the view isn't half bad, I thought, stealing a glance at the grumpy man beside me.

He turned a raised eyebrow at me, and I gave him my friendliest smile. He rolled his eyes and laid back as though trying to sleep.

"I take it you didn't mean to say that out loud," he said.

Damn. This was going to be a long flight.

CHAPTER THREE

Rowen

"... AND A BEEF FOR YOU," THE STEWARDESS SAID, handing me a tray covered in foil, as if it were a delicacy.

I accepted her offering and unwrapped my plastic cutlery, ready to dig in.

We had been in the air for two hours, and I knew from experience that mealtimes were the only thing that broke the monotony of magazines and bathroom breaks on long-haul flights. I peeled back the covering to reveal two slices of meat swimming in gravy with soggy vegetables beside it. The dinner roll was warm, at least, and the butter melted. Score.

"I'm so sorry, sir, we've run out of the beef. Is vegetarian okay?"

I glanced to my left, where Mr. Grumpy side-eyed my tray briefly before nodding tightly at the bearer of bad news. She leaned down more than strictly necessary to place his meal on the tray in front of him.

"Nice rack," I murmured irritably.

For all she knew, Mr. Grumpy and I could have been traveling together. Unprofessional is what it was. Grumpy snorted as the stewardess straightened and moved on to the next row.

Peeling back the foil on his meal, my seatmate grimaced at the sight of a mix of roughly cut, soggy vegetables swimming in a tomato sauce. The desire to watch him struggle through a meal that he obviously didn't want was strong, but the potential to make a friend for the long-haul flight had me moving before I realized I had made the decision.

Lifting my meal, I slid his vegetable nightmare to my tray and replaced it with the beef and gravy. Without looking at him, I picked up my fork and speared something that may have been a zucchini at some point. I could do this. It all looked the same in our gut, anyway.

Closing my eyes, I popped the unidentifiable object into my mouth and was pleasantly surprised to find it was just as bland as the meal I had sacrificed in the hopes of friendship.

Overhead, the seatbelt sign flicked on with a ping, and the pilot announced a spot of turbulence, asking that passengers return to their seats. After three bites, when I could feel his stare burning into the side of my head, I raised a brow at him in question. He met my eye with a forest-green gaze that drew me in, even as those eyes narrowed at me in suspicion.

"Eat your meat before it reverts to its natural cardboard state. It's really hard to chew when it's ninety percent tree."

He smirked, and I hated myself for looking away first. I was winning, damn it, but Mr. Grumpy was even more attractive when he smiled. We ate in silence as the airplane bounced around intermittently. As I sopped up the last of my tomato juices with the bread roll, a sigh came from beside me.

"Thank you. I hate tomato."

"No problem," I said, hiding my grin.

"I'm Jett, by the way," he said, awkwardly twisting his arm to offer a handshake.

"Rowen."

Jett was a sergeant in the Army. Was I smug that I'd already guessed that? Uh, yeah. Of course. He was headed home for three months' leave to see his family and reconnect with his girlfriend. He answered every question I had openly and with humor.

The eldest son of a retired colonel, he had followed his father into the services, but refused to get a commission because "officers never get to have fun". He spoke at length about his younger brother, who had gone into a corporate job at home, and how he would have to drag him out of the office to kick his ass in their annual surfing competition.

In return, I avoided all questions about my own family, but told him plenty about my friends, my vlog, and the adventure I was setting out on. He called me crazy more than a few times, and I laughed at his total lack of plans for his trip home.

"You don't have anything planned?!" I asked at one point.

"Nothing," he said, grinning. "Sun, sand, and friends. That's all I need."

It sounded nice, but I would still have wanted to do more with so much free time.

When the pilot announced we were coming in for a landing, Jett shook me awake from where I slept, drooling peacefully on his shoulder.

"Sorry," I muttered, swiping at the wet patch on his t-shirt.

Worn out and in desperate need of a shower, I still felt a thrill of excitement at having reached our destination. As other passengers jostled to get to their baggage, I fired up my phone and opened my camera. I looked less than photogenic, but I wanted to get my first vlog out so I could enjoy everything this destination had to offer.

Jett plucked the device from my hand and snorted at my squeak of indignation. "Don't worry, I have steady hands. Tell me when to record."

I stared at him for a moment, shell-shocked. No one had ever offered to film for me. No one had taken my vlog seriously enough to offer any kind of help, really. Outside of sponsors, who would pay as little as possible to profit from my endorsement and the exposure I could provide.

He's taken, I reminded myself before I could go completely goo-goo eyed.

Fluffing my hair, I pasted on a grin and nodded to Jett. He furrowed his brow, and a moment later, I heard the small beep of the camera activating.

Taking my cue, I threw my hands up dramatically. "Hey, babes! It's been a long haul, and I've already made friends. Give a warm welcome to our celebrity cameraman, and we can get along with the clue for our first mystery destination."

I winked outrageously at the camera before leaning in and dropping my voice. "I got lei'd as soon as I landed, and now I'm off to dig my feet into the beautiful black sand beaches. Watch where you step, though, you don't want to erupt. Where am I? You know the drill, react and comment, and I'll pin the answer when I post the next clue! See you in twenty-four hours, my loves, and remember... you only live once, so live chic!"

I kept my smile in place as I frantically waved at Jett off camera to stop the recording. He chuckled, handing my phone back.

"Well, that was something. What did you mean you got laid?"

The passengers beside us started funneling toward the front of the aircraft, and Jett gallantly blocked the path with his body so I could slide out and grab my bag. The jostling of people as we disembarked meant that the next time we could speak was as we came out onto the tarmac.

"I always feel like one of the old school celebrities when I get off an airplane this way," I observed as I adjusted my grip on my bag.

"Of course you do," Jett said, snatching my bag and swinging it over his own shoulder.

"But imagine it. Big sunglasses, flowy dresses, walking inside and being handed a cocktail, lei around your neck while waving off paparazzi. It would be awesome."

"If by awesome, you mean a nightmare. And don't expect any of that to happen."

"Are you telling me we won't get leis when we hit the arrival lounge? Bummer."

We bantered back and forth as we made our way indoors and finally headed through to the arrivals lounge. No leis, damn it, but there were a ton of people. One woman was holding a sign that made me choke in vicarious embarrassment. In large black letters was the message, "I'm having Felix's baby. Fuck off back to the mainland."

"Oh, shit. I'd hate to be that guy," I said, nudging Jett and pointing blatantly at the sign.

It took me a couple more steps to realize he had stopped. His face turned a weird shade of green.

"What's wrong?" I asked, backtracking to grab his elbow in concern.

He cleared his throat once and then a second time. "That's my girlfriend," he breathed.

Shit. "And Felix?" *Shut up, Rowen. It's none of your business.* But I couldn't help myself. I liked this guy. We'd just spent a great eleven hours getting to know each other.

"My brother." Oh, yeah. I should have remembered that.

"Shit."

CHAPTER FOUR

Rowen

"I'M AN ASSHOLE, AND I'M SORRY," JETT RUMBLED A second before he hooked an arm around my waist and smashed his lips to mine.

It's all for show, I reminded myself frantically as my body relaxed into his, the kiss all heartache and desperation. It was for a purpose, and I got it. I fucking got it. No one should be broken up with via cardboard sign at the end of a long flight. None of the self-talk stopped me from threading my fingers through his hair and opening up beneath him.

Damn, this guy was a good kisser. Clearly, that chick was out of her ever-loving mind. His tongue pressed against mine as he kissed me so hard our teeth clicked together. His soft, warm lips worked over my own. Though his hands stayed respectfully still, I couldn't help wishing they'd wander a little as my body heated, and I forgot why we weren't supposed to do this.

An unholy shriek cut through the best make-out session I'd ever had. Our lips parted, and Jett shielded my body as the cardboard sign came down across his shoulders, seemingly having been turned into a weapon by an irate cheating girlfriend.

"Ow! Kylie, quit it. What the fuck?" he groused, blocking the next strike with his forearm and scowling at the small woman in front of him.

"How dare you bring this trash around here! How dare you flaunt her in front of me while I'm pregnant!"

Jett pinched his nose as the crowded terminal quieted to witness our drama.

"You wanna go ahead and read your sign again? Then you can tell me why you think you would get any say in what I do anymore." His voice was low and even, and maybe I was already worked up from the kiss, but I couldn't deny it was definitely doing it for me.

Kylie swung the cardboard at him again as two security guards materialized out of the crowd. Taking another blow to the arm, Jett moved in front of me and looked at the two guys. With a quick nod, they disarmed Kylie and led her away; her screaming insults and profanities echoing in the large space.

"That was hot," I breathed without meaning to.

Jett huffed a laugh and turned back to me as the crowd lost interest in us and returned to their own reunions.

"Welcome to Hawaii." He held his arms wide and took a step back toward the baggage claim. This was it. We'd talked through hours of flight time, he'd decimated me with one kiss, and now it was time to say goodbye.

Unless...

"Hey," I called as he turned to walk away. He froze, and I hurried to get in front of him, watching his face intently.

"So, I know you had super big, important plans for your time off."

He snorted.

"But do you want to come on an adventure? I can find all sorts of shit to get us in trouble for. Like, all over the world. Fuck her, and fuck Felix, too."

He was going to say no. I didn't know what had come over me. Eleven hours had been enough, and he was going to yell at me for saying fuck his family, and—

"Yes."

I blinked.

"Did I just have an aneurysm? Because I thought you just said yes."

Jett grinned, and this time, I was sure something short-circuited in my brain.

"I did say yes, idiot. Why not? I'm a single guy now. I could spend my entire break in jail for beating the shit out of my brother, or I could protect your ass from possible murdering scammers. Plus, I'm pretty good with a camera."

I was not falling in love with a man on the rebound. I swear.

Damn it.

***

A last-minute ticket purchase and a few greased palms meant we had no problem securing Jett's spot on my flight from O'ahu to Hilo.

One hour and twenty minutes later, we were flying down the road in a cherry-red Mustang with the top down.

"It's beautiful," I muttered, watching the bright greens and earthy browns of the Hawaiian rainforest flash past as we wove our way toward the national park.

I had argued for stopping at the house I found on Airbnb, but Jett insisted we could swim after visiting the national park and relax through the afternoon before our flight in the morning, because *who comes to Hawaii and doesn't see a volcano?*

I had to admit; I was excited. This was my first time leaving New York state. Growing up, whenever I asked to travel, my mother would sniff and ask what I called our summer home in the Hamptons. Apparently, a chance to show off how much money we had was not the right answer.

My parents had never been interested in anything unless there were influential people present to fawn over them. If I were honest with myself, this trip was long overdue, and despite the excuse I used to take off, I was enjoying myself. My family's money allowed me the freedom to travel. I was aware of my privilege, but being in a different place, with the chance to see a different culture? It was everything I ever wanted.

"Hey, let's go back to O'ahu and go to a luau tomorrow," I said.

Jett frowned. "I don't know if that's the best idea. You already put the vlog up early; you don't want to give them a chance to catch up. Plus, why would we go to O'ahu when there are plenty of luaus here?"

I flushed, realizing most of my knowledge of Hawaii came from T.V. shows that always seemed to be set in Honolulu. No way was I about to admit that level of ignorance, but it was a good reminder to check my assumptions about other countries.

"The chance anyone is actually after me is small. I'm sure the flowers thing was a fluke. Come on, let's enjoy the trip and make some good content," I said, spotting a sign for the national park.

Pulling into a parking spot, we waited silently as the roof came slowly back up over us. The crease between Jett's brows deepened, and I reminded myself I didn't care how he was feeling about recent events.

I couldn't be attracted to this guy; he just broke up with his girlfriend. I was the random, crazy new friend who was planning on dragging him all over the world; not his rebound fling. My lips tingled in denial. Damn it. Hoping to curb any further progress down that mental path, I threw myself out of the car.

The Kilauea Visitor Center was full of amazing information about volcanoes and the goddess Pele. Jett snorted as I paid for my book on the goddess, but wisely kept his mouth shut. He was good company. He hadn't said much since the incident at the airport, but quiet seemed to be his way when he wasn't teasing me. I realized I wanted him to stay for the rest of this adventure, which immediately made me wonder how long he would last before he got sick of me and took off.

Pushing the inevitability aside, I concentrated on a fascinating tour of the park and had almost completely forgotten the catastrophic idea of returning to traveling solo by the time we made our way back to the parking lot.

"I love it here," I said dreamily, once again watching the landscape pass by my window.

"You might have mentioned that a time or two."

I punched Jett in the arm as he slowed the car to take a bend in the road. "Don't be a..." The words died in my mouth as the jungle parted and I glimpsed the sparkling blue waves spread below us.

"You wanna stop?" he asked.

I nodded mutely, unable to look away from where the water washed over honest-to-god black sand.

The second he parked the car, I was out the door and picking my way down the steep slope to the shore. I tore my shoes off, dropping them in my rush to get to the water, and dove in fully clothed.

It was glorious. My hair swirled around me as I lay back and drifted, staring at the brilliant blue of the afternoon sky. This was what I had needed. Freedom. A shadow passed over me, and I looked over to find Jett waist-deep beside me.

"Umm... Where is your shirt?"

He chuckled, and the movement tightened his exposed abs into a freaking eight-pack. A black tribal design stretched from his heart up and over his shoulder, weaving around the bulge of his bicep, and I had to swallow to work moisture back into my mouth.

Friend. He's a friend, Row.

Despite the mental reminder, my eyes drifted down over the V at his hips and settled on the waistband of black boxer briefs, which were clearly the only item of clothing he'd left on.

"Not all of us like to hang about in wet clothing, you know. Easier to swim in boxers, then take them off to put your clothes back on."

"Are you saying I should have stripped down to my bra and panties to swim? Jett, we just met."

I could have sworn his eyes heated, but then he glanced around us, and the moment was lost.

"Look, I don't think it's a good idea to stay in the islands for too long, but we can go to a luau tonight, okay? Just promise you'll tell me before you post anything online. Deal?"

"Deal."

CHAPTER FIVE

Sullivan

"When are you coming home?"

Rayleigh's voice was barely audible in my Bluetooth earpiece as I strode into the early evening, the heat of the day still emanating from the tarmac of the private airstrip. Slung over my shoulder, I carried a black duffel containing the tools of my trade.

"I've one quick thing to do and I'll be home. How's Mam today?"

Ray rattled off a list of drugs and doctor's orders that no eight-year-old should be able to recite, let alone carry out, and I swore to myself that after I finished this job, I would find a different way to keep the family afloat. Something more legal that kept me at home so Ray could have a goddamn childhood.

Blade shouldered past me with a sneer that I returned twofold. I hated the guy. Honestly, I hated most of the guys I had to work with, but money spoke loudly enough that I'd play nice for at least a little longer. With more than a little gratitude to get out of the heat of the dying sunlight so quickly, I followed him into an open hangar and looked for a place to set up my computer.

"Maith thú, well done," I muttered absently, carefully unpacking my laptop and bringing up my tracking software.

I was no hacker, but compared to some of the guys I had been teamed with in the past, I was a fucking guru. Tracing people wasn't an overly complicated task if you had the right gear and basic computer knowledge, and it was this knowledge I used to confirm the target was definitely still on the island. That was helpful. I could get the job done quickly, get paid, and maybe have time to catch up with an old friend for dinner.

"Sully, you aren't listening to me!"

"I am, Pet, I promise. You're doing an amazing job with Mam. I'm sorry I'm not there."

"Where are you, anyway?"

I hated lying to Ray, but it wasn't safe for her to know the details of how I kept our family afloat, so I kept things as close to the truth as I could.

"I'm visiting Linden. Do you remember him?"

The squeal that met my disclosure seemed somewhat disproportionate. Ray had liked Linden when she met him a couple of years earlier—everyone liked the smooth-talking surgeon with a heart of gold—but this reception?

"Oh em gee! You're in the same country as Living Chic! Sully! What if you ran into her? You could meet her!"

Ray gushed over the internet star for some minutes as I checked and rechecked my equipment for the mission. Cable ties, tranquilizers, rope... I ticked each thing off my mental checklist as I ensured each piece was in top condition. A glance across the room proved Blade was also doing equipment checks. Knives, rifle, handgun... that couldn't be right. Muting my call, I gestured toward the pile in front of him.

"This is catch and release. Why the fuck does it look like you're going to war?"

Blade grinned. "I got different orders. Fuck off and mind your business."

Did he have a second assignment on the island? Fuck him. Hopefully, he screwed it royally so I wouldn't have to work with him again. He was way too affectionate with those blades, if you asked me. Intimate in a really creepy way. Anyway, he was right. None of my business, as long as it didn't affect me and mine.

"... she saved me, y'know?"

I tuned back into Ray, noting the change in her tone of voice.

"What?"

"Living Chic. I know it's a stupid dream for you to see her. I know how big the island is, but I first saw her on a day when

Mam was bad and you were away, and it was so nice to pretend to be a normal girl for a minute. So I started watching her channel. She posts super regularly, and it's just a minute or two when I can learn about something that is nothing like our reality."

My chest ached at the age in her voice. This. This was exactly why I needed to finish this job, get paid, and work out how to be the son and brother I needed to be.

"I'm glad you have something that helps."

"I'll send you her vlog. She's the best. Maybe she can help you, too."

A sharp whistle was all the warning I had that we were moving out. Dick that he was, Blade needed me for this assignment.

"Sounds great, Pet. Hey, can I call you later? Love you, *a pheata*."

"Love you too."

Ray ended the call first, as always, and I smiled as my phone immediately buzzed with a text.

"Talk to your girlfriend later, Irish. Time to hunt," Blade said, cranking the engine on the black SUV, which was every cliche wrapped into four wheels.

"It was your mam. She said you need to find your own dinner because she'll be eating my dick." I swung into the passenger seat and slammed the door just to piss him off.

He didn't bother responding to my jibe, but I could hear his teeth grinding as we idled in the growing dark. I grinned, hoping he would see it. Knowing he would cave.

"Will you just tell me where the fuck we're going?" He usually lasted longer, but the long flight had clearly worn him down.

I continued to stare patiently out the windscreen. In the field, I was the consummate professional. Transit on the way to a job, when I knew we were going to be early, anyway? Yeah, I'd make him sweat it out a bit more, just for my own amusement. The dashboard lights were the only source of illumination, and they lit just enough to show Blade flex his hands repeatedly on the steering wheel.

Finally, he sighed without looking over. "Would you please give me directions?"

"See, that wasn't so hard now, was it?"

I was tempted to pat his shoulder; however, being fond of my fingers, I decided against it. Instead, I gave him directions to a hotel that sprawled across a cliff side, overlooking the ocean as though awaiting a lost love. So what if I was a closet romantic? The place was nice, was all I was saying.

On the grounds beside the building, there was a stage set with tiki torches, lighting lines of crowded tables and benches. A short way off, a pair of guys in matching shirts fussed over what looked like some kind of smoking pit.

Ray would love the atmosphere of this place, I realized as I watched people move around, getting drinks and talking to performers in grass skirts and flower crowns. At the thought of my sister, I moved a little way away from Blade and discreetly pulled up the link Ray had sent me.

A bubbly, cheerful voice filled my Bluetooth speaker as I got the impression of fair skin and bright blue eyes. Her rosebud mouth pulled into a smile as she spoke about... I didn't know what. I had stopped breathing.

With a hand that trembled more than it should for a seasoned bounty hunter, I pulled up the photograph I had received of the mark. The red hair had clearly had a recent cut into the shoulder-length shag in her video, but there was no doubt.

The woman who had reportedly given my baby sister the only reprieve she asked for in this miserable life and the woman I was here to abduct were one and the same.

Rowen Black.

Shit.

CHAPTER SIX

Jett

WHAT THE HELL WAS I DOING? I HAD TAKEN LEAVE TO repair my failing relationship and had somehow ended up single and agreeing to travel the world with a woman who may or may not be in trouble with some criminal elements. She didn't seem worried about the whole thing, but considering the security she described in her building and how it had been bypassed? I supposed time would tell.

The woman in question was grinning like a mad thing while up on stage learning how to hula. She was so carefree. A cynical part of me wanted to point out life was easy when you could afford anything, but that wasn't fair. The hours we'd spent together proved that while she was naïve and definitely sheltered, she didn't take her money for granted.

Another part of me wished I had that kind of financial freedom as the box in my pocket burned deeper. I had hoped someone might steal it during our impromptu swim, but no such luck. Kylie and Felix. I felt so stupid. Kylie had always been a fan of my brother. I had even encouraged them to spend time together while I was deployed in war zones, fighting for our country's freedom.

While I waded through the blood of my brothers—obviously not Felix, but those who fought by my side—I found comfort knowing Kylie was safe. Even if I hadn't survived, I knew she would be cared for.

Apparently more than I had expected.

I knew I was partly to blame. When the only thing you had to talk about was death and survival; silence was an excellent option. Kylie spoke about nail appointments and how we could spend the money I was making. It was all so trivial I wanted to scream some days.

The obvious solution to me had been to go big and give her what she wanted. The largest rock I could afford and a promise to put a down payment on the house she had seen go up for sale.

An email had come through on my phone earlier responding to my enquiry, but I hadn't worked up the balls to open the thing yet. Not their fault my life had done a one-eighty, but I couldn't think of a nice way to say my brother fucked the girl I was buying the house for.

A problem for another day.

I tried to relax into the atmosphere of the night. It had been years since I last went to a luau, and I was looking forward to diving into the kalua pork when dinner was served.

Rowen's laugh drifted to me from where she chatted with a couple of local dancers, pulling my unwitting gaze to her again. She was, quite possibly, the most charismatic person I had ever met. Stunningly gorgeous, from her red hair to her oddly long toes, but that wasn't it. She exuded happiness and inspired a confidence in humanity in me I thought had been extinguished at gunpoint years ago.

By all rights, after the day I'd had, I should have been three sheets to the wind in a dive bar somewhere in the back streets of Honolulu. Instead, here I was wondering why something seemed off about the night.

Swiping a hand across my neck to ease the prickling feeling, I swept a covert eye around the gathering. Tourists crowded long benches. Their garishly colored shirts and sunburnt faces, neon signs labeling them as visitors to the islands.

On the edge of the light, a tall redheaded man dressed entirely in black stood beside a dark-haired man in matching attire. Each had a black bag slung loosely over their shoulder. None of this was overly suspicious. They could have been security, but in my paranoid mind, they seemed to stare in Rowen's direction.

Moving slowly, I left my seat and ambled over to the woman in question, who appeared to be convincing a tourist to film her dancing with a couple of employees in traditional garb. She grinned as I approached and thanked the people around her, moving to meet me halfway.

"Having fun?" I asked, glancing briefly at the company she'd just left to see if they glanced toward the suspicious characters I'd noticed before.

No one else seemed to pay them any mind. Seemed that either I was paranoid, or the men weren't part of a wider conspiracy. At this point, I couldn't have said which was more likely.

"So much fun. You should have danced. I'm sure you can move those hips when you need to."

The red that stained her cheeks when her words registered was the kind of attractive I wasn't ready to acknowledge. Even as I had to clear my suddenly tight throat.

She was not some rebound girl. I knew that without a doubt. She deserved more than a recently single cuckold who had known nothing but death and sand for the last three years of his life. I could, however, be her friend and keep her safe from threats, both real and imagined.

Maybe the psych evaluation had been accurate, after all. I'd never considered myself a candidate for PTSD, but if I was jumping at shadows... it was definitely a good time for a break.

"These hips are better at other things. You hungry?" I pretended not to see her double take, but couldn't help the smirk that crossed my face once I turned my back.

We headed toward the long tables at the back of the clearing where workers laid out plates piled high with food. At her request, I explained some of the more traditional dishes and convinced her to try poi on her pork.

As we took our seats, I cast another quick look toward the odd men out, only they had disappeared. Good thing? Unsure. Maybe I had been mistaken from the beginning.

With a shake of my head, I dug into my meal and enjoyed watching Rowen discover new culinary delights.

After a few more drinks, I started looking for a restroom. "Hey, can you stay here? I'll be back in a minute," I said, noting the port-a-potties near where we left the car.

Rowen waved me off, deeply engaged in the conversation she was having about pineapples with the ten-year-old beside her. Fuck, I didn't want to leave her.

Moving quickly, I headed out of the circle of light toward the cliff, where the makeshift restrooms sat. My pocket buzzed, reminding me there was life outside of this crazy adventure I had embarked on.

Answering without looking was my first mistake.

"Where the fuck are you? Mom's worried, and Kylie—"

"Kylie can go fuck herself. Or, why don't you do it for her? I've got nothing to say to you right now, Felix," I interrupted.

He scoffed. "Really? You're going to get upset about that? Life goes on, Jett. You left her here alone and you expect her to just wait for you?"

I was sure he could hear my teeth grinding down the phone line. "I was trying to stay alive, defending our country, while she fucked my brother and spent my money."

"Please. More of that self-sacrificing bullshit? She knows you had a month's leave over summer. You chose not to come home."

"I was in hospital with a shrapnel wound, you fucking prick. It was rehab, not fucking R-and-R." Was I shouting? Screw that. He wasn't worth the energy.

My brother had always known how to get under my skin. Add in a complete disdain for my career choice after we grew up in the Army brat lifestyle, and I knew I would get no empathy from him. I never thought he would actively help my life go to shit, though.

"You know what? You deserve each other. Have a happy life and leave me the fuck out of it."

Ending the call, I shoved the cell into my pocket and looked out over the cliff, using the deep breathing techniques I had picked up from my physical therapist when I had made it abundantly clear I wouldn't be accepting any kind of mental health support. Maybe I had completely lost my mind.

I watched the waves wash over the shore below me for a moment, then with a final deep breath, completed my trip to the urinal. I made quick work of the facilities and was drying my hands when I noticed an unusual quiet had settled outside.

"What...?"

Bang.

Instinct had me hitting the deck before the fact I had just heard a gunshot at a luau registered. The sound was so foreign in the setting that some would write it up to a car backfiring, but I knew better. And I had a good idea of who the target was.

Rowen.

Throwing the door open so hard it bounced and almost caught me on the backswing, I vaulted out of the small cubicle.

She had to be safe. I told her to wait. But how many people with a viable threat against their life could be at one luau?

Backlit against the moon rising over the sea, a dark shape slumped on the ground close to the edge of the cliff. It rose against the skyline and resolved itself into what looked like a tall person carrying something suspiciously human-shaped.

They took off at a run, and I followed at full speed, instinct screaming that I had failed.

"Hey!" I shouted, closing on the figure. This close, I could see they were definitely male and of similar stature to the redhead I had marked earlier.

At the sound of my voice, he startled and increased his speed toward the parking lot.

I cursed, diving as I got close to take him out at the ankles. We fell in an inelegant heap, a deep grunt coming from my prey as the body he was holding rolled out of his arms.

"She's shot, you idiot. We don't have time for this." The voice had an unfamiliar Irish brogue that wouldn't sound so pretty when I was finished with him. Getting my feet under me, I prepared to attack when his words registered.

She. Was. Shot.

Fuck.

I looked past his hulking mass and noted long pale limbs sprawled unmoving in the dirt.

"Rowen!" I yelled, scrambling forward to roll her face up.

My hand came away sticky, and it didn't take a genius to work out that it was from a bloody patch spreading like an ink spill across her shirt.

"We have to get her out of here. You're wasting time." The Irishman was back, and he wasn't giving up.

"Who the fuck are you?"

"I'm the reason she's injured and not dead," he replied, far too calm for my taste.

But he was right about one thing; we didn't have time for this. Pressing two fingers to Rowen's throat, I found a weak pulse and felt the slightest loosening in my chest as I scooped her into my arms and strode toward our rental car.

"I'm coming with you."

"Like hell you are. You've done enough. Fuck off before I make the time to deal with you."

Despite being taller and bulkier than me—which was saying something—the prick was light on his feet as he danced alongside me. "Anyone tell you, you cuss a lot?" He moved out of the way as my foot glanced off his knee. Damn.

"I'm a bundle of fucking sunshine when my travel companions aren't dying in my arms. Fuck. Off."

"I highly doubt that." He reached into the Mustang and opened the way for me to place Rowen inside with a shit-eating smirk. As though he hadn't had a hand in her current condition.

Stepping back from the car, I turned, following through with a fist that left the asshole out cold in the dirt as I tore off toward the one person I could trust to save this girl I had just met.

CHAPTER SEVEN

Linden

"... REGRET TO INFORM YOU, THE BOARD HAS RETURNED their decision. You are to be placed on unpaid leave pending further investigation into the events leading up to the death of Mr. Allicott on blah, blah, blah."

I screwed up the letter outlining my new position as a scapegoat for the incompetence of the Honu Mahalo Hospital, the grinning turtle letterhead mocking me until I drop-kicked the thing into the wall.

Maybe my time in Hawaii was finished. I had been thinking of taking a trip. Maybe doing some volunteer work with one of those charities in third-world countries. Rediscover my passion for medicine.

I chuckled morbidly to myself. Fuck that. It would take a miracle to bring the passion back. Possibly, I was just older than my years and needed to move to LA. Specialize in cosmetic surgery where money was good and I could run my own practice.

Even the thought caused bile to rise in my throat.

The buzz of my cell caught my attention just as someone started hammering at my front door. Leaving the call to go to voicemail, I opened the door to a face I hadn't seen in years.

"Jett?"

"No time. I need your help. Do you still have emergency gear here?"

I stepped aside, gesturing for him to come in. "Yes, I..." I trailed off as he turned and bolted toward a red convertible idling in my driveway. "Jett?"

"Help me with her."

That got my attention. I jogged down the front stairs to meet him as he dragged a limp figure—female?— from the backseat.

"Bullet wound to the lower left torso. Unconscious on discovery, slow heartbeat. Non-responsive for the last fifteen minutes. Tell me you can help her." Jett was spitting out stats better than any of the nurses in that godforsaken hospital I was possibly no longer employed by as he carried her carefully into my lounge and deposited her on the sofa.

"I can't do it in here. Bring her through to the back," I said, mentally running an inventory on what I would need and what I still had at hand. Although I was less than proud of the fact I had a side hustle patching up those who operated outside of the bounds of the law, it came in handy when old Army buddies came to call.

"What the hell happened?" I asked as I quickly scrubbed in, glancing over my shoulder at the unconscious woman laid out so carefully on my table.

Jett sighed and pushed her hair back off her forehead in a gesture that seemed overly familiar, seeing as the last time we'd spoken, he was still seeing that Kylie chick.

"We were lulled into a false sense of security after she had a threat made on her life." He looked up, and the shadows in his eyes were darker than I'd ever seen them. "I fucked up. I was supposed to be watching out for her."

I snapped on some gloves and grabbed a pair of forceps and scissors to cut her shirt away from the wound.

"That's not your usual gig. Did you transition into private security when I wasn't looking?"

"Hilarious. No... it's complicated. I'm on leave and sort of fell into the job." He swiped his hands over his jeans, shifting from one foot to the other.

"I'm going to need boiling water for sterilization."

I didn't need boiling water, but I knew too well the hopelessness that came from not being able to contribute to an outcome you were invested in. Keeping him talking, keeping him busy, would be the best thing for him until I could get the girl stitched up and on her way to recovery.

With an economy of movement, I ran an IV line with a bag of fluids before turning to the wound. In the time it took for

Jett to return with the boiled water, I had cleaned the wound, located both entry and exit points, and confirmed there were no residual elements of the bullet left in the cavity. Amazingly, the trajectory had missed all vital organs, meaning her chance of a swift recovery without complication was high.

"You didn't need this at all, did you?"

I smirked at the growl in his voice as he stood awkwardly in the doorway with a large saucepan of water.

"You don't know her blood type by any chance, do you?" I asked instead.

Blood was one thing I couldn't keep in stock, but I could procure it if I needed to. The shake of his head was unhelpful, but expected. I stitched the wounds, closely monitoring my patient's breathing. The most concerning part of the surgery wasn't so much the hole in her side as her continued unconscious state.

"Did she take anything tonight? Were you guys drinking earlier in the evening?"

Jett shook his head again, brow creased as he stared intently at her face. "She had a cocktail, but it was one of those shitty little plastic cup deals at the luau, and I watched her drink it. No chance of tampering. Someone tried to abduct her, though, so it's possible she was drugged. Why would someone shoot her if she was already unconscious?"

It was my turn to shrug as I took my patient's vitals again and confirmed she was stable, if unresponsive.

After dressing the wound and ditching the soiled gloves, I was scrubbing my hands when another hammering started up.

"What is going on tonight? Stay in here. Whoever it is, I'll get rid of them."

Jett nodded and closed the door to my makeshift operating room as I once again made the trip to the front of my house.

"Sullivan," I greeted my guest with a hand to his chest as he tried to push past me.

"What brings you here?"

"Is she ok? Did she get to you in time?"

His shirt was wet beneath my fingers, and now that I looked, I noticed his face was too pale. Fuck. Clearly, he was involved in all this somehow. I fisted the fabric under my fingers and pulled him inside, slamming the door as I turned to face my sometimes-friend.

"What exactly do you have to do with the unresponsive woman in my back room?"

"She's still out?" he said with a frown. "I thought she would have been awake by now." A retching sound came from the back room, closely followed by a whimper.

I narrowed my eyes at him. "Sevoflurane? What the hell is going on?"

A small amount of color returned to his pallid face as he let out a long breath. Striding across to my sofa, he sank down, pushing the heels of his hands into his eyes and scrubbing hard.

"It was supposed to be a bag and tag. Nice and clean, but then shit got complicated."

"Complicated how?" I asked. I could hear the exhaustion in his voice, but the noises from the back room were bleeding my empathy dry.

"She's Rayleigh's favorite influencer. She's been making my sister's day a little less shitty, and I'm supposed to fuck that up for her? I couldn't do it."

His hands dropped to his sides as though he couldn't hold them up anymore. The house grew quiet. The girl's vomiting hopefully stopped for now.

"So what happened?" I asked, leaning in the doorframe and wondering what the extent of the chaos was that had come to my door.

"I decided to change up the plans. I was going to miss the rendezvous and get her somewhere safe, but it turns out Blade's orders were different to mine. Jesus, or maybe he went rogue? I knocked her out like we planned, but then he pulled a gun. It was supposed to be a bag and tag," he repeated, looking up at me through red-rimmed eyes. They widened slightly just before I was knocked on my ass by a furious blonde tank whose sights were squarely set on the bounty hunter in front of me.

"I'll show you a fucking bag and tag," he growled, driving his fist into Sullivan's face with so much force that it was a shock the man was still upright.

"Jett," I said, torn between vindication at seeing someone punished for what happened to the poor woman and the need to know the whole story.

I let him get one more swing in before pulling him off the Irishman. It occurred to me as I threw Jett into a chair across the room that Sullivan hadn't even lifted his hands in self-defense. His remorse seemed genuine as he eyed the back room and ignored the blood dripping from his nostril.

When I was satisfied Jett would sit still, at least in the short term, I turned to the matter at hand.

"Tell me the rest. How did you know to come here?"

Sullivan wiped the blood from his lip with the back of a hand and grimaced. "I was going to bring her here myself, but... ah... I tracked her cell. Anyway, so there I was, I had just knocked her out for transport, and Blade pulled a gun, the fucker. I tried to throw her out of the way, but my hands were bloody when I shot back, so I knew she'd been hit. As soon as he was down, I booked it, and then this idiot took me out."

"Nice try, asswipe, but there was only one gunshot," Jett snarled, gripping the arms of his chair tight, as though ready to launch himself across the room.

"Yeah. My weapon. His had a silencer. Clearly, I missed the memo on the change in job description. I'm a bounty hunter, not a fucking assassin. I don't kill people."

"Yeah? Well, I do."

I caught Jett as he made a move for Sullivan again.

"Not in my house. Are we clear? The important thing is she's safe. I need to check on her, but I do not want to see any more blood spilled in my house. It's a bitch to get out of the furniture."

Jett lifted his lip, ready to test me, but deflated after another long moment of eye contact.

"Good choice," I murmured as he flopped back into his seat. "How about you both get cleaned up and I'll see how our patient is doing."

CHAPTER EIGHT

Rowen

SHIVERS WRACKED MY BODY, AND MY STOMACH FELT like the time I got drunk on root beer floaters and Long Island Iced Teas. My head pounded as I tried to remember how the hell I had ended up in a room that looked vaguely like a veterinary clinic.

I was lying on a metal table, and my first round of vomit still splattered the linoleum floor. If it wasn't for the fact Jett had been with me until two minutes ago, I could've imagined I'd been kidnapped by black market dealers who wanted to take my kidneys and leave me in an ice bath.

Actually, an ice bath sounded wonderful, I thought as I reached for the bucket Jett had found for me to vomit into.

We were becoming fast friends if we were already at the sharing bodily fluids stage. Actually... scratch that. We weren't sharing any fun bodily fluids. He was just kind enough to help me manage mine. Also, I clearly had to remind myself that my newly single travel companion was friend-zoned. He'd been through enough shit recently, and now it seemed I was dragging him into more.

The door slid open with a soft whoosh, and I winced as bright, white light invaded the dim space.

"Sorry. Here. Is that better?" A smooth, deep voice floated through the room as the door was closed again.

I sighed as darkness was restored and uncovered my eyes to track the newcomer. He was tall, easily as tall as Jett, with dark skin that blended with the dim light in the room. He moved to a basin in the corner and wet a washcloth.

"You're safe here," he said, moving slowly toward me, cloth held out like an offering. I accepted it with a still trembling hand and wiped my face and neck.

The cool, damp fabric slid across my skin in a blissful caress that cleared my mind of the fuzziness I'd awoken with.

"Thank you...?"

"Linden. And please, no thanks necessary. I wish we were meeting under different circumstances. Are you comfortable? Do you need some painkillers?"

I grimaced as I sat up, holding my side tightly. "Do you have anything that won't make me drowsy? No offense, but I haven't known Jett long enough to take his word that you're trustworthy. Especially after being shot and apparently drugged."

Linden nodded and flashed bright white teeth in a stunning smile before turning to one of the many cabinets that lined the room.

"I'd recommend oxycodone, considering you've just been shot and had minor surgery, but I understand how you're feeling, so I'll let you choose. Would you prefer codeine or ibuprofen?" His voice was calm and confident as he pulled several boxes out and lined them up along the counter. It was clear from the way he moved that this was his safe space.

"Did you do the surgery?" I asked.

Curiosity won out over suspicion as he moved methodically around the room, drawing a glass of water for me and placing it with the selection of pills before leaning casually against the wall. His shirt sleeves stretched over his biceps as he crossed his arms in a way that hinted at a fit body beneath. This man was beautiful—Idris Elba level gorgeous —and I knew my priorities were all messed up while I admired the coffee color of the skin on his cheekbones in the dim light as he jerked a sharp nod.

"So you're a doctor?" Of course he was. Make him even more attractive, damn it.

Another nod.

I leaned back on my hands with a slow, outward breath. "Then I'll trust you to give me the right thing."

His eyebrows twitched, but with another nod, he became all business as he shook a couple of pills from an orange bottle and offered them to me with the glass of water.

I only hesitated a moment, then swallowed them quickly. My side was aching, and I was keen to find out exactly what had happened to me. Jett had only told me someone shot me, but we had made it to a safe place, before male voices in the other room drew his attention. The way he stomped out hadn't boded well for whoever was out there. Clearly, it hadn't been Linden who worried him, seeing as he was still in one piece.

Finishing the glass of water, I slid from the edge of the bed and only had a moment to realize my legs wouldn't hold me before Linden was there, supporting me with gentle hands. He slid his shoulder under my arm and helped me through the door and out into a beautiful sitting room where two men sat on opposite sofas.

Jett glowered at a huge redhead I had never met before. When I said huge, he was easily the biggest man I had ever seen, making the two-seater sofa he sprawled in look like a children's play table. His nose was slightly crooked, and there was a touch of blood in his left nostril, but he appeared completely unconcerned. Neither by the darkening bruise on his left cheekbone nor the hostility coming off the man across from him in waves.

I cleared my throat, suddenly parched despite the water I had just drunk, and two sets of eyes swung toward me. Both men leaped to their feet, and a silent staring match ensued, during which Linden guided me to the nearest seat and settled me in a nest of throw pillows so I could sit up comfortably.

"Sit down. Both of you. Sullivan, start talking. Rowen deserves to know why you drugged her and almost got her killed." Linden's voice was considerably colder than it had been a moment ago as he addressed the giant.

Sullivan flinched, but didn't protest as he sat and scrubbed his hands together as though trying to conjure the words.

"I am not a good person," he started.

Jett grunted, and Sullivan shot him a glare.

"I am not a good person," he said again, eyes narrowed on Jett. "I've been a bounty hunter for more years than I care to admit, but I am no assassin. When Blade shot you, I'd already gone rogue. Think what you want, blondie, but it's true."

Jett clearly didn't believe the man with the beautiful Irish accent. He sat back with a huff and crossed his arms firmly. I shot him a quelling look before turning my attention back to my would-be kidnapper. Or was he still my kidnapper? My head was starting to pound in sync with my side. I knew I should have accepted stronger painkillers, but this was important.

"So what changed between the time you accepted the assignment and you went rogue?" I asked.

"It turns out you may have saved my sister's life."

"I... what?"

He told me about his sister. About his Mam and her sickness. Unflinching, despite being in a room with men who clearly didn't like or trust him, he opened up and told me everything. Jett didn't seem inclined to believe a word he said, but I had a feeling Jett didn't trust much.

"So you have no idea who hired you?" I asked when Sullivan seemed to run out of steam.

"Not how it works, *a pheata*. The *powers that be* send the assignment, and when it's complete, we get paid. These people are dangerous, though. Have you any idea how you ended up on their radar?"

I shook my head slowly, thinking hard. "I didn't send them the money they asked for. Maybe I shouldn't have messed with them."

"Money means nothing to these people. Have you done anything else that could've drawn their attention? You come from money, right? Have your parents pissed anyone off?"

"Are you kidding? They would do anything to be the most liked people in the world. No way anyone has a beef with them. They're just about to launch some charity thing in a couple of months, and everyone who is anyone is stuck so far up their asses that I'm not surprised no one recognizes half of what they say is shit. They care about appearances. That's it."

A brassy ringing interrupted my well-rehearsed parent rant, and I startled as Linden crossed the room to a rotary telephone that I would have put money on being an antique. After offering a polite greeting, Linden's face went blank for a moment before he offered the receiver to me.

"Hello?" I asked tentatively, unsure who could be calling a complete stranger's landline to speak to me in the middle of the night.

"What the hell is going on?" Makenna barked at me over the connection.

"How did you know where I was?" I had no clue how to answer her, and with Mak, the best defense was always a good offense.

The sigh that came back at me down the line was all frustration.

"Your cell pinged in the same place for the third hour in a row, and you didn't answer when I called. I hacked the security feed in the parking lot."

Huh. I hadn't noticed cameras when we were there, but Mak was scary when she was on a mission. Her aunt's neighbor's dog was baited once, and she managed to shut down a dogfighting ring while bringing the offender to justice.

"Anyway, I followed the car through the traffic cams and the good doctor you're staying with lives at a busy intersection. He seems like an okay guy, but there are some bank transfers that don't add up. How did you meet that dude, anyway?"

I choked on a laugh as Mak casually listed the number of federal offenses she had committed because she was worried about me.

"Basically? I almost got kidnapped, and then I got shot. Wait... maybe I did get kidnapped. Wait." I looked at the three men watching me closely. "Am I kidnapped?"

"Of course not," Linden said at the same moment Sullivan yelled, "No!"

Jett grunted. He didn't seem inclined to go out of his way to talk around the others. Grumpy bastard.

"Anyway, Jett brought me here to get patched up. We're behind schedule, and I'm going to have to go find my cell so I can upload the luau video. Can you book my next flight?"

"I want Jett's full name and social security number," Makenna announced at the same time Jett growled, "Book us."

"Right. Um, flights for Jett and me?"

"You literally just had surgery, Rowen. You need to stay under medical supervision. I recommend you take a few days of rest before you take off," Linden said gently, leaning forward in his seat.

"She can't do that. We need to get to another country as fast as possible. The more we move around, the safer she'll be. I'm not the only person who was sent after her," Sullivan said.

"What do you mean 'we'? There's no fucking way you're coming with us," Jett growled, moving between Sullivan and me as though ready to kick his ass if the big guy even thought about breathing wrong.

"I already told you. I owe her a life debt. I failed at my first try, so now I'll be sticking with her until the threat has passed, or she herself has told me to fuck off."

I tried to remind myself it wasn't actually about me. These guys were using me as a reason to have some kind of a dick measuring competition. I couldn't deny it was hot, though.

"Rowen, tell him to fuck off and we'll head out," Jett ordered without breaking the stare down.

"I'm considering everyone who volunteers for tickets as having provided formal consent for me to do a deep dive into their lives. No one is hurting you on my watch," Mak announced down the line.

"Rowen, you really need to rest," Linden pointed out again.

"Rowen—" Sullivan started.

"Enough! Geez! Mak, can you book four tickets on whatever flight is leaving in the next two hours? Whoever wants to come will have a seat, and anyone still arguing can stay here and tug on their dicks for all I care.

"Mak, investigate whoever you want; just don't get yourself in trouble. I can't take that on my conscience. I want to go and get my cell. Now. I love you, and I'll call as soon as I have it back. Kisses." I hung up the phone, marched to the door, and stood, arms crossed, trying not to sway on my feet as my side ached, while I waited for them to make a decision.

"Fuck. She's something else, isn't she?" Sullivan muttered.

Linden shook his head and crossed to where I stood. "If you insist on leaving, I'm going too. You need someone to keep an eye on your wound."

"Don't you have a job to think about? I can keep her safe, and I know enough to monitor her recovery," Sullivan said, breaking away from Jett to clap Linden on the shoulder.

"Not anymore," Linden said, glancing at a wastepaper basket in the corner of the room, then walking out into the night.

"Okay, so the unemployed doctor, the dashing bounty hunter with a death wish, and the soldier are heading out on an adventure to save an influencer heiress. This should be interesting," Sullivan observed lightly before sauntering along in Linden's footsteps.

"How the fuck do you know I'm a soldier?" Jett called after him. A snort was all the answer he got.

"So what do you say?" I asked tentatively. Despite the short time we had known each other, there was something comforting about Jett's grumpy disposition. I didn't really want to do this without him, but I also didn't want to force him into anything.

"I'm not leaving you alone with him. God knows what his agenda is. You want me? I'm yours. Let's get your cell back."

I stood frozen on the stoop, watching as the men piled into our rental, still bickering.

Friend-zoned, I reminded myself.

It felt less true every time I said it.

CHAPTER NINE

Sullivan

"I DON'T CARE IF IT'S ACCURATE. THEY WILL USE ANY means possible to track you. I disabled your GPS, but if they're wasting time trying to get visas to a country you're not in, we can get some breathing room to come up with a better plan," I argued with the firecracker in front of me.

She was such an interesting mix of confident, entitled, and honorable. Cerulean eyes narrowed at me and she all but stomped her foot on the threadbare carpet of the departures lounge we were passing the time in.

"My followers expect integrity from my content. How can I tell them I'm somewhere I'm not? What if someone calls me out? I can't keep lying. My parents are liars, not me."

"What if you don't specifically say you're there? Just give the hint and don't elaborate. You have your content and integrity, and Jett and Sullivan can keep you safe." Linden pierced me with a look I didn't appreciate but begrudgingly accepted.

Jett and Rowen didn't know me from Adam, and I hadn't proven myself trustworthy yet because fucking Blade was quick with a handgun. It hurt that Linden thought so little of me, though. I'd known him for years.

I couldn't exactly tell them I wasn't in the habit of hurting people I was attracted to either, both because I had—in fact —hurt her, and I didn't think she needed the extra stress of another man showing interest. Although she seemed completely oblivious to our other travel companions' covert glances.

"Great idea, Lin, we'll do that. Here, give me your cell and I'll film for you," I said, hoping I sounded enough like a team player for Linden to drop the finger-pointing.

"That's my job," Soldier boy growled from three rows down where he was pretending to sleep.

"Oh no, I wouldn't dream of disturbing you. Trust me, you need all the beauty sleep you can get," I said, smothering a grin. This bear was going to be fun to poke.

"Keep teasing him and you're going to lose 'big bad' points," Rowen warned me as Jett flipped me off without opening his eyes.

I grinned, slipping Rowen's cell from her back pocket and cueing up her camera. Her squeak of protest was everything. Somehow, despite all that had happened tonight, she wasn't scared of me. I really didn't want her to be scared of me.

"Remember the clue we agreed on?"

"I didn't agree to anything. I told you I didn't want to lie."

"Excellent. I'm going to live stream you in three…"

"Wait."

"Two…"

"I'm not—"

"One."

Her smile was instant and dazzling as she switched effortlessly into her 'Living Chic' persona.

"Hi, babes! It's your girl, Living Chic, coming to you with the next installment of Where in the World! If you missed the gorgeous footage I uploaded earlier, then I'll confirm for those who may not have guessed—I'm in Hawaii! I've had an amazing time here, but now we're moving on and you get to guess our next destination."

The tiniest flicker at the corner of her mouth let me know she was exceedingly pissed at me, and I held my breath, momentarily doubting the wisdom of forcing her into this the way I had.

"With a flag that looks like it could provide first aid, these friendly islands are worth a look! Get your detective hats on, my loves, and see if you can catch me out before I post the answer. Until then, remember, you only live once, so live chic! Love you." She blew a kiss at the camera, and I shut down the connection.

The second I lowered her cell, she snatched it from my hand with a scowl that would have been frightening if it weren't so damn cute.

"You did the right thing," I told her gently.

"I still feel dirty. I'm giving a real hint from the next country."

"After we leave," Linden pushed.

"Yes! After we leave. God. You guys are so freaking bossy! Chill out."

The chime of the PA announcing our flight was ready to board interrupted me before I could start another rant about her safety. Was I being overprotective? Yes. I had a shitload to make up for, and I knew damn well what the monster under the bed looked like. She still didn't seem to grasp exactly how much danger she was in.

"You need to keep away from her. She may not care who you are, but I'll be damned if I let you fuck her over," Jett growled at me as Rowen and Linden joined the line for boarding.

I sighed.

"Does she know you're in love with her yet?"

His face shut down so quickly it was comical. Yeah, dude had caught some serious feels. I wondered if Rowen reciprocated them. I had caught her looking at all three of us, but maybe I was seeing what I wanted to see.

"I just got out of a long-term relationship. Not that it's any of your business, but I'm not in love with anyone."

"Excellent, then you won't mind if I get to know her a little better."

I dodged his fist and headed toward check-in, forcing a laugh around the twinge in my chest. Jesus. I didn't deserve her, but I didn't know if I could stay away.

Linden took the seat beside Rowen, which meant I ended up spending the nine-hour flight cozied up beside the grumpy soldier. It was a long-ass flight, made longer by the periodic giggles coming from across the aisle where Linden was apparently providing Rowen with riveting anecdotes. Fucker.

By the time we arrived at our next destination, I was plotting ways to make the others take a nap so I could spend some time with the girl.

I wondered if I could convince her to say hi to Ray and decided it couldn't hurt to ask. My sister would most likely deafen her, but then maybe it could keep her from getting into trouble for a hot minute.

"Bienvenue," a hostess said with a smile as we passed through the arrivals lounge. "Profitez de votre séjour ici."

"Merci," Rowen replied without missing a beat. Fuck, I hoped people spoke English here as well. We were a long way from Paris.

"What did she say?" I asked, looking around the terminal as though I had better things to do than hear the answer.

"She wished us a pleasant stay, you cretin. You're from Europe and you don't speak French?" Linden asked with an evil glint in his eye. I knew exactly what he was doing, but national pride forbade me from keeping quiet.

"I'm from Ireland, thank you. We don't even like to acknowledge Britain. Why the fuck would I care about the rest of Europe?"

Rowen chuckled and headed toward the baggage claim, but not before I caught her pressing a hand gingerly to her side.

"She's in pain. Why haven't you given her anything for it yet?"

"She won't let me. I'm hoping when we find a hotel, she'll take some painkillers and a nap before she goes out exploring. She's rather willful, isn't she?" Linden's face was full of admiration as he watched her trying to tug her bag off the carousel. I took a step toward her just as a shoulder check threw my balance off. Jett flipped me off behind his back as he jogged over to assist Rowen.

Child.

Were we all seriously going to compete for her attention? I palmed my cell and thought again of Ray. Yeah, we definitely were.

***

A cloud of diesel smoke belched from our shuttle as we chugged into our hotel for the night. *Hotel was an understatement*, I realized as we walked into a five-star reception area and learned we were going to be staying in over-water bungalows for the night.

"They're not secure," I argued as we walked along the wooden boardwalks that connected all the suites.

"Oh, don't be such a bore. No one knows we're here, and when are we ever going to be in Tahiti again to get the chance to sleep in one of these things? This has been on my bucket list for years. I'm going to have to find a crazy good Christmas present for Mak after this."

She pushed into the middle of three bungalows that had been booked under the name Makenna Fairburn and gasped, "Oh my God! Look at this! I can see fish!"

The bungalow was a single room with a large canopied bed, a small kitchenette, and discrete ensuite with a huge spa bath inside. The wall facing the water was glass with a sliding door out to a deck with an outdoor shower and a ladder into the crystal-clear water. I didn't know how much of this Rowen had taken in because she stood, entranced, staring at a section of glass flooring at the foot of the bed that showed schools of brightly colored fish swimming below.

"Let's go for a swim," she announced suddenly, turning and holding her hand out to Jett for her bag.

"You shouldn't get that wound wet," Linden countered, slipping into the room with a deep frown creasing his face.

The way Rowen's chin tilted told me my friend would have a fight on his hands. At least it wasn't me in the bad books for once. She may be sweet and kind, but Rowen did not like being told no.

Backing quietly out of the room, I left them to square off in favor of finding a Wi-Fi connection. There was still a major threat out there, and I was going to monitor the situation closely until I could neutralize it once and for all.

In the main building, I hit the jackpot, finding complimentary computers for guests. Plugging my cell into the port, I logged into my Hawaiian proxy server and uploaded the software to access my employer's case file on Rowen.

Blade had reported in, and my profile had been tagged as rogue, kill on sight. Great, an added complication there, but at least they still had the watch location set for Hawaii.

Blade's most recent update had him querying a visa for Tonga. Even better. Blade was a psychopath, but he was the 'work smarter, not harder' sort, and I knew for a fact he'd underestimated Rowen's intelligence.

I should have killed the bastard while I had the chance, but I was working under the theory that if Blade was still in play, at least I knew who we were dealing with.

"Reporting in to your bosses? I fucking knew we couldn't trust you."

Jett's hand came down on the back of my neck like a fucking hammer. With a grunt, I threw my elbow back to break his hold and glared at him.

"Checking in on the status of the threat, dickhead. You'll be happy to know they bought the decoy. You're fucking welcome."

Jett muscled in next to me, clearly disbelieving as he inspected the screen.

"Be my guest," I sniped, refusing to move an inch to accommodate him. He inspected the flight plans, progress reports, and other miscellanea of documents outlining the logistics of making a person disappear.

"What's this?" he asked after a while.

"Just a time log," I said, ready to close this shit up. The longer it was open, the more susceptible we were to a counter hack.

"No, the time log was built into that other file. This is different."

Shit. He was right. The file seemed innocuous, but as soon as I started digging, it became obvious the encryption on the coding was far more complex.

"Fuck. I can't break this. What is it?"

"Sure, you can't," Jett said, sarcasm heavy in his voice.

"I'll do whatever I need to keep her safe, no matter what you think," I muttered, investigating the code.

How had I missed this? And why was it buried? There were too many things that didn't add up in this mission. I would never have forgiven myself if I'd completed it. Even if this ended with my body in a landfill, at least I knew going rogue had been the right decision.

"What do you think it is?" Jett asked, moving closer to the screen. As though proximity could help decipher what we were looking at.

"Nothing good, but definitely something we need to get into. Problem is, there's only so much we can do. I have basic hacking skills, surveillance shit mostly, but nothing like what we'd need to get in here."

Jett grunted. How he managed to make his grunts expressive was beyond me, but he was very clearly giving me a 'what the fuck good are you, then?' grunt. Asshole.

"Rowen might have more of an idea, or maybe her friend can help," I said, done with his company and keen to get back to the girl in question.

Without waiting for his permission, I started the shutdown procedure while Jett huffed and scoped out our surroundings. Once I could disconnect my cell without announcing our location to the world, I switched off the computer for good measure and headed out into the heat of the day.

Stupid sun.

There was a reason I preferred to work at night. I didn't have a good complexion for sunbathing, and the idea of a burn was about as much fun as telling Ray I was almost part of killing her favorite influencer. That conversation was going to blow.

Squinting against the glare, I skirted the hotel's wading pool and beelined toward the boardwalk out to our bungalows. No one was in the water nearby, and I wondered if Linden had convinced Rowen to take a rest. Sleep would do her good, and honestly, at least I'd know she was healing.

If the circumstances weren't so dire, I'd have her on a flight to Ireland with me, wrapped in cotton, so I knew no one could cause her harm ever again. Fuck, how had she dug under my skin so quickly? I didn't want any of this near my family, but the idea of her meeting Mam? Meeting Ray? There was an awful lot of appeal if I allowed myself to imagine it.

I breezed past the first cabin and opened the door to the middle one, stopping short and grunting when Jett collided with my back. The bungalow was empty. With an order to

Jett to check the first cabin, I jogged to the third and found it untouched. Where the fuck were they? Back outside, I could tell from the scowl on Jett's face his inspection had been just as fruitless.

Rowen was gone.

CHAPTER TEN

Rowen

I KEPT MY CAMERA STEADY AS I STEPPED INTO THE giant hall that held tables and tables of different wares for sale. Behind me, I could still hear Linden grumbling about leaving the others behind, but I needed some time away from the dick-swinging, chest-thumping, alpha male bullshit. I was a strong, independent woman, and as much as I appreciated them trying to keep me safe—and the bossiness was a turn-on—I still wanted to see the world.

"Did you at least leave them a note?" Linden asked, ruining my shot of a beautiful hand-woven grass skirt. I huffed and stopped recording.

"Of course I did. Don't you think they would have found us already if I hadn't?"

Thankfully, Linden didn't seem the sort to push. It wasn't the most responsible route, seeing as there were people out there trying to kill me, but I got a kick out of the idea of those two tough guys finding a note that simply said: *Gone shopping, back when I want. Stay.*

"I can see you grinning, and I don't want to know. As long as I'm not going to walk face-first into a gun when we get back," Linden said, watching me from the corner of his eye.

"How about I go in first? That way, I'll have the gun in my face and you have plausible deniability," I said, noticing a little old lady with a beautiful flower crown on her head who was selling woven bags and baskets. Before Linden could bitch further, I wandered over to watch as she took a bunch of dried grass and began to deftly bend and thread the strands around each other.

"That's amazing," I whispered as first the base, then the sides of a basket took form.

Linden stood quietly by as I watched her finish the piece, then urged me farther into the markets. We saw fresh produce and homemade wares, hand-sewn clothing, and counterfeit goods and movies.

"Didn't this just release in theaters?" I asked in wonder, picking one title out of the spread.

Linden chuckled and drew me toward a fresh fruit stall.

"Try this," he said, offering a slice of a smooth, slightly slimy looking pale orange fruit.

"What is it?"

He held it to my lips, and as I sucked the fruit into my mouth, his eyes flared. The buttery sweetness hit my tongue with a slightly tangy aftertaste that was almost as delicious as the sight of Linden licking the juice off his fingers. My belly warmed as I saw his pink tongue flick out from behind plump brown lips.

Down, girl. No attacking the doctor.

He paused, thumb in front of his mouth, and smirked. "Hungry?"

I snapped my eyes away from the glistening digit and cleared my throat loudly. "Umm. Just a bit bored, I think. What else should we do?"

His chuckle told me he didn't believe me, and when he put an arm around me to guide me through the crowd, I didn't protest.

After the markets, we visited the pearl museum, where I bought a beautiful white gold necklace with a large Tahitian black pearl inlaid pendant. Criss-crossing the island, we entertained ourselves with the sights until the sun began to set.

Linden's cell had gone off incessantly until he answered it and agreed to twenty-minute check-in texts and quick phone calls on the hour as 'proof of life'. Seeing as both the guys were on speaker each time I spoke to them, I had no idea whose bright idea that had been.

Rather than find a fine dining restaurant, I convinced Linden to eat under the stars, surrounded by food trucks and locals laughing and talking animatedly in French. It was freeing to sit anonymously in a crowd of people going about their daily lives. I could barely understand enough to order dinner, but smartass Dr. Smooth had us covered.

I almost came from hearing him order chevreffes and poulet fafa. Why did I have to be surrounded by sexy men who were all out of bounds? *There's only one way to deal with the tension*, I decided as we finished our meal.

"We're going dancing."

Linden looked up from his poe, one eyebrow arching in question. I wasn't about to admit I was going to look for a hook-up—we were due for a check-in phone call and the last thing I wanted was the others to know what I was planning —so instead of elaborating, I just shrugged. Linden mirrored my gesture and returned to his dessert.

***

Dark room? Check. Loud music? Check. Alcohol? Linden turned away from the bar and handed me a mocktail. I scowled up at the responsible doctor and received a shrug in return. "You're on meds."

The dance floor was already heaving with bodies, and I could feel the music working its way through me, urging me to move. Sipping at my drink, I let my eyes roam over the crowd. Searching. Was this even a good idea? Probably not, but I wanted one hour where I didn't have to be the scared girl running for her life.

I wanted to be free.

To dance when I wanted, fuck who I chose, and forget anyone who had a problem with it. We had checked in with home base—as I had insisted on calling it, much to Jett's disgruntlement—so the clock was ticking. Leaving Linden on the sidelines, watching a muted sports game on the screen over the bar, I dove into the crowd and let the music take over.

As I moved, I side-stepped couples staggering over each other and deftly dodged groping hands. Close to the stage was exactly what I was looking for. I hoped. A man who looked a little younger than me danced with wild abandon to the music, as though the throbbing bass had him in a thrall. He was tall, with long lashes brushing high cheekbones as he kept his eyes closed to the world.

Just as I decided I couldn't intrude, deep brown almond-shaped eyes flashed open and caught mine. He grinned and held a hand out, inviting me into his space, and I went. How could I do anything but follow? Pin straight black hair fell across his forehead as he ducked his head to yell in my ear.

"Zephyr."

I grinned.

"Rowen."

And then we danced. I let out a laugh of sheer joy as we moved in sync with the beat. Fast and slow. Complex and simple. Until we were both sweating profusely and smiling so hard it hurt. I knew I would pay for it later, but I was in a pleasant kind of numb where my side didn't hurt in the slightest.

"Can I get you a drink?" he asked, taking my hand and leading me from the floor.

"Rowen." Linden appeared at my elbow, a frown creasing his brow.

"I need this," I said simply.

I couldn't decipher the look that crossed his face—it was gone too fast—but just in case, I pushed up on my toes and kissed his cheek. It was meant to be his cheek, anyway. His head turned toward me and I found my lips at the corner of his mouth. His warm breath fluttered across my cheek, and my heart hammered as I lowered myself. Grabbing Zephyr's hand, I took off toward the back of the building like a coward.

Down a dark hallway, near the washrooms, was a storeroom with its door standing slightly ajar. Pushing it wider, I turned and fisted Zephyr's button-down shirt. "Kiss me."

His smiling mouth crashed to mine in a wild and passionate frenzy I hadn't been expecting. His hands cupped my face gently as he pressed me back into the wall beside the doorway.

"You're beautiful," he said in between kisses as he brushed my hair away from my eyes.

"I want you to fuck me. Okay?" I replied, feeling awkward at the praise and keen to get moving before anything could go wrong.

His face morphed comically from shock into enthusiastic joy as my words registered. I barked a laugh and pushed him through the open doorway as a shadow passed across the end of the hallway.

"Rowen," Linden called, striding toward me as I froze in my tracks.

"I'm not trying to be an asshole here, but I need to keep you safe. The others will literally kill me if anything happens to you."

"They will not," I replied automatically, although Linden probably knew both men better than I did.

The thought was a sobering one and the exact thing I was trying to avoid. So I did what I did best: I went on the offensive.

"If you're so worried about my wellbeing, you have two options here. You can stand sentry and make sure we're not disturbed... or you can join us." I kicked my chin up and waited for him to back down from my challenge. Or just call and rat me out to the others, honestly. I wouldn't have blamed him for either action... much. Instead, he stilled.

"You want me?" His gaze bore into me, and part of me could acknowledge this had been building all day. Hell, it had been building for the last two days since I'd woken up in his house.

"Yeah. I mean, because you... do? If... I mean, if you want to?"

Smooth, Row. Real smooth.

As I fumbled through a proposition which was nothing like the one I had just offered Zephyr, my would-be lover poked his head out of the storeroom.

"Oh, cool. Hey, dude, are you joining us? Or you want me to leave?" His face was open and keen, and it was at that moment it occurred to me that I had decided to have a threesome. With two strangers. In the back of a nightclub.

And there was nothing I wanted more.

With a deep breath for courage, I smiled up at my travel companion, injecting as much sass as I could into my words.

"Linden's just deciding if he'll join or not."

"Get your ass in that room," he said, eyes so dark they looked black in the dim light.

I squeaked and bolted through the doorway, straight into Zephyr's arms. He swept me up effortlessly and spun me into the back wall, crashing his lips to mine as I registered the click of a lock turning. A second click flooded the room with light, and I pulled away from Zephyr's kiss, head swimming in a potent mix of lust and excitement.

Linden stood, back to the door, watching us as he unhurriedly slipped his shirt buttons open one at a time. His face showed a cool interest, betrayed only by the tenting of his chinos. Zephyr glanced over his shoulder and grinned at the sight that was heating me up so much.

"What do you want us to do, boss man?"

Linden cocked his head at Zephyr, eyes glinting. "You're like a puppy, aren't you?"

Zephyr chuckled. "Not the first time I've been called that. Won't be the last, either."

"Rowen. If you're uncomfortable at any time, I need you to speak up. If I ask you a question, I need to hear the answer. Understand?" Linden punctuated his question by slipping his shirt off his shoulders to display the hard muscles of his arms and torso.

I may have swallowed my tongue. Knowing he expected an answer, I nodded, my eyes traveling down to the grooves in his hips that disappeared beneath the waistband of his pants.

"Words, Rowen. We can play in a minute."

"Yes," I said, snapping my eyes back to his.

The smirk that crept across his face dripped seduction, and I gasped as I subconsciously moved against Zephyr's rigid length, where it pressed into my core.

"Good. What's your name, puppy?"

"Zephyr. Now, are we going to talk all night? Or can I start making her feel good?"

Linden laughed, a short sharp sound that told me Zephyr had surprised him. "Ok, puppy has teeth. How about you use them to strip our girl, here."

In the next moment, I was on my feet and facing Linden, where he continued to laze against the door as though this were a normal occurrence for him. Hell, maybe it was...

The depressing thought was cut short as Zephyr swept my hair back from my neck and trailed small bites and kisses along my collarbone toward the shoestring strap that held my sundress. I shivered at the brush of his lips as he eased down one strap and then the other. Next, he bent and eased the zipper down my back, his nose tickling the skin along the way.

The dress dropped in a billow of fabric, leaving me in a pair of panties. I hadn't bothered with a bra because it was hot, and there wasn't much to support, anyway. My parents hated me going anywhere any less than perfectly dressed and made up, so maybe it was just another rebellion that I continued to enact against my 'proper' upbringing.

"Are you okay?" Zephyr's voice floated up from where he kneeled, and the brush of his fingertips told me he had found my wound.

"It's fine. See? All patched up," I said lightly.

He wrapped a hand around my hip and pressed his lips to the bandage in a sweet kiss that almost made me combust. A girl could only take so much.

"Your lips are in the wrong place, puppy. How about you make her feel better?"

Linden's voice was so low, I could have sworn I felt it vibrate in my pussy. Fuck, that was hot. Zephyr hummed in agreement and ran a hand up the inside of my leg, urging me to widen my stance with a soft touch.

"Eyes on me, trouble," Linden said.

I watched as he palmed himself through his slacks at the same time Zephyr stroked me through my panties. Groaning obscenely, I rocked against his palm as he worked his fingers in teasing touches over and over until I was soaking wet and frustrated as hell. When I was ready to scream at him, Linden called a stop.

"Shoes off, panties off. Puppy, how are you with your tongue?"

I didn't see the response, but strong hands removed the last of my clothing and bent me at the waist until I was eye to eye with Linden's crotch.

"You're going to suck me while he fucks you with his tongue. Would you like that?" he asked, slowly unbuckling his belt.

I nodded.

Linden's eyes flicked over my shoulder, and a hand came down hard on my ass. Squealing, I shot a scowl over my shoulder at the man who was now lavishing my burning ass with kisses.

"I remember the rules. Do you?" he asked with a cheeky grin.

I wondered briefly if he had any other expressions.

"Yes, of course."

"Good," Linden said, lowering his zipper and guiding his thick head to my lips.

There was barely enough room for us to situate ourselves. As I started to move on Linden's length, he swung his hips subtly to keep me as still as possible while Zephyr speared me with his tongue.

My moan was lost around the heavy cock Linden buried in my throat as Zephyr worked me with an expertise I would not have expected. My first orgasm hit me so hard I gagged. Linden caught me by the shoulders, holding me through the aftershocks before nodding at Zephyr over my shoulder to continue.

After my second climax, Linden shuffled aside and encouraged me to brace myself on the door for two more. My body was jello by the last one, and I whimpered as Zephyr stroked my ass cheek affectionately.

"This was fun," he said as Linden's hands appeared to support me to standing.

"But... what about you?" I asked, struggling to focus through the dopamine coursing through my tired brain.

"Neither of us has condoms, and you need sleep," Linden said firmly, leaning me against the door and accepting my dress from Zephyr.

I held my arms up as he slipped the fabric back over my head and settled it in place. Kneeling before me, he slipped my shoes on one by one before straightening and pocketing my panties.

"What...?"

"These are mine now," he said with a wink.

Confused, satisfied, and still slightly turned on, I followed the men out of the room. At the end of the hall stood an emergency exit, propped open with a cement block. Opting for the quick exit over the heaving masses, we stepped out into the night as Linden's cell buzzed.

"You want to answer? I don't feel like listening to death threats right now," he said, handing me the device as he led us toward the road to find a cab.

Accepting the call, I put it gingerly to my ear.

"Hello?"

"Where the fuck have you been? You're forty minutes late for check-in. Put Linden on the phone. A text saying you're fine isn't what we agreed to."

The irate Irishman was loud enough through the call for his voice to echo in the mouth of the alley we were leaving, and Zephyr flinched.

"Stop yelling at her or we're going to have problems." Jett's growl was a balm, and I was surprised by the relief I felt at knowing both of them were still there.

Sullivan snorted. "Like we don't already. Fine. Please, Rowen, will you come back to the bungalows so we can see for ourselves you are safe and not in the hands of my former employers?"

A white taxicab pulled up to the curb, and we piled in as I continued to reassure the men I was, in fact, fine.

"We're heading back now. I'll see you in ten minutes, okay?"

They agreed, but refused to end the call until I was walking down the boardwalk toward them.

"Who the fuck is that?" Jett asked, eyeing Zephyr with suspicion.

"We picked up a stray," Linden said, not breaking stride as he took my elbow and steered me around the gathering and into my bungalow.

"Show me your wound. I want to make sure it's okay after this evening's... activities," he said, leading me toward the bed and urging me to lie flat.

Before he could lift my dress, the door burst open, bouncing off the wall as an angry redhead filled the threshold.

"Why didn't you answer? You had very clear instructions for check-in. For all we knew, Blade had finished the fucking job and we were waiting on a corpse."

"Sullivan," Linden warned.

"No, he's right. We had an agreement, and I didn't honor it. I'm sorry for worrying you," I said, reaching for Linden's hand. He laced his fingers easily through mine, and Sullivan's eyes snapped to the connection.

"Right. So you put her at risk to get your dick wet. You remember she was shot yesterday, yes?"

"Of course I remember. You were the one who got her shot. I just patched her up." Linden's voice was cool, but I felt the tension through his fingers.

In the distance, I could hear the low rumble of one voice and the energetic response of another, indicating Jett and Zephyr were at least partly getting on. The water lapped against the bottom of the bungalow, and as the silence stretched between the guys, I felt suddenly tired.

"You know what? My wound feels fine. I think I'm going to get some sleep now. So if you want to keep fighting, can you take it somewhere else? Tell Zephyr he can stay in here if he needs somewhere to crash."

Without waiting for a response, I crawled under the covers and pulled them to my chin.

"Thank you for today, Linden."

Both men mumbled a goodnight and filed out of the room. I considered getting out a nightshirt or something, but it seemed like too much effort. Footsteps tapped outside the door as the men headed away from the bungalow, and just as I was on the edge of sleep, the door opened again.

Two figures slipped into the room, treading lightly as though worried I'd wake up. The first moved to the small sofa, sitting with a grunt that told me Jett wouldn't leave me unprotected. The second slid between the sheets on the other side of the queen bed I lay in.

A hand slid across the distance and squeezed my fingers gently before retreating, and I let the last piece of tension disperse, knowing Zephyr had decided to stay. For how long? I didn't know, but at least we had the night.

CHAPTER ELEVEN

Jett

A DEEP GROAN WOKE ME FROM A LIGHT SLEEP IN THE predawn hours when the sun threatened the weary with the hint of a new day. One thing that was definitely up was my cock, which had clearly registered the noise we were hearing before my sleep-addled brain.

A second groan came from the bed, and I was awake enough to identify it as feminine. My cock leaped at the sound. Fuck. I should have left. Should have feigned sleep, but instead, I used the shadows I sat in to watch.

A mound under the blankets at the bottom of the bed moved rhythmically as Rowen's breath caught in her throat. It was the kid, Zephyr, and he was doing a fucking good job of licking pussy if the noises Rowen was making were anything to go by.

My throat tightened, and the urge to rip him out of the bed —to take his place—was almost overwhelming. A soft, keening cry came moments later, and I wasn't sure if I was happy it was over, or disappointed I hadn't joined in.

Zephyr crawled up the bed, and they spoke in whispers. I closed my eyes, forcing myself to tune it out, and somewhat succeeding, until I heard the subtle slide of a drawer followed by the familiar crinkle of a wrapper.

Unable to resist, I found myself watching the pair as she rose over him. The light from outside fell perfectly on the bed, highlighting the beautiful couple as he lifted her dress over her body and let the garment fall to the floor. Her pale skin glowed, mesmerizing me as she began to ride the lucky prick beneath her.

Fuck, she was glorious. Her hair brushed her upper back as she tossed her head in ecstasy. The slight hint of breast I could see bounced in time with her hips.

This is not for you. I squeezed my cock hard, hoping for some relief, and had to stifle a groan of my own. I squeezed again, harder, and as the couple began to lose inhibitions, I gave in and began to stroke.

Feeling like a creeper, I bargained with myself. *Just until I don't feel like my balls will explode. I'm not going to finish right here. I'll stop in a minute.*

I didn't stop.

Rowen came with a scream that covered the sound of my own groan as I pumped hard into my boxers. Zephyr moaned his own release, and everything went quiet. Slitting my eyes, I feigned sleep as the couple decided to shower. As soon as they were locked up in the bathroom, I headed out to find new clothes and bathe myself.

The fact I didn't feel dirty in the aftermath was not something I wanted to think about.

Linden launched a pillow at me as I pushed into his bungalow, turning on the light so I could search my bag for fresh clothing.

"Turn the goddamn light off. What time is it?"

"Shower time. Fuck off."

Linden flipped me off, face buried under his second pillow, as I made my way into the ensuite. I left the light on just to fuck with him.

Turning the shower on as high as it would go, I stripped out of my clothes while I waited for the water to heat. Jesus. I hadn't come in my pants since I was a teenager. Balling the soiled mess tightly, I kicked it into a corner to deal with later.

We were going to have to find a laundromat wherever we went next. I knew some of us had endless access to funds, but the rest of us would need to wash shit. Especially seeing as Sullivan had had to borrow shit to wear today. How long could we keep this up?

I stepped into the steaming water and immediately considered blasting the cold tap as images of what I had just witnessed played out in my mind's eye. The scalding water was Rowen's hands, her body all over mine. I was the one pulling those noises from her with my fingers, my tongue, my cock.

I fisted my erection, unsurprised it was back and as painful as it had been. In my mind, Rowen didn't treat me like a friend who was on the rebound. If I were honest, my relationship had been over for a long time. Kylie never made me feel this out of control.

When Rowen and Linden missed check-in the night before, I had been as worried as Sullivan. More so. We had agreed not to mention to Linden we'd bugged his cell before they left. I wouldn't be surprised if Sullivan had bugged mine too. It didn't bother me. If he was the enemy, I would just dump my cell on a bus and let him chase his tail around the island while I got Rowen away safe.

Rowen. I couldn't focus around her, and for that reason, I was grateful I had the others helping to keep her safe. Even if I didn't trust them completely. Thoughts of the other guys deflated the erection I had no right getting, so I took a moment to scrub myself clean and turned the water off.

I was pulling a pair of jeans over my ass when the door behind me flew open and a fucking overgrown leprechaun grinned at me.

"What the fuck, man? What if I was taking a shit?"

Sullivan smirked. "Well, that would've been embarrassing for you. Pack up, we're moving out. Oh, and I borrowed another shirt."

He was wearing the smallest shirt I owned, and I noted how it stretched over his shoulders, the tight fabric highlighting his abs. Fucker was trying to get noticed.

Of course he was. We all were. Except only fucking Zephyr —and I had a suspicion maybe Linden—had had the opportunity to get close to her so far.

"Why are we moving so early?" I asked, grabbing my shirt off the counter and shoulder-checking him on the way out of the bathroom.

"It's go now or be stuck here. Shit's going down and we don't want to be here when it does," Sullivan said cryptically.

I was starting to know Sullivan well enough to tell when to push and when to leave it. This was one of the latter times, so I shrugged and started shoving things in my bag.

"You told Rowen?"

"She's busy showering with her new boy toy. Is he coming with us?" Sullivan asked.

I shrugged. The possibility we were adding yet another to our group hadn't occurred to me before now.

"Trust me; the puppy is smitten. He'll be coming," Linden grumbled from the bed.

"Get your arse up and get ready to leave. I thought doctors were good with no sleep," Sullivan said, pulling the covers from the bed. Huh, the dude slept in boxer briefs.

"I am running a constant sleep deficit because I'm a doctor. We sleep where and when we can. Now is a time when I'm supposed to be sleeping."

"Do you want me to send Rowen in to wake you up? Boss you around a little?"

I grinned, happy to see Sullivan screwing with someone else for once. The good doctor groaned long and loud, then dragged himself out of bed.

"I'm not going anywhere without a long, hot shower," he said before slamming and locking the bathroom door.

"Not a morning person, huh?"

Sullivan chuckled. "I turned up on his doorstep with a stab wound at five A.M. once. He almost stabbed me a second time for waking him up."

"I'm sure it was all because of your charming nature," I said, hoisting my bag over my shoulder.

Sullivan scratched his chin. "Yeah, could've been that... or possibly the fact I threatened to break in and bleed over every surface of his home until he made the bleeding stop, or I ran out of blood." He shrugged. "One of the great mysteries of life, I guess."

Damn. The fucker was funny. I wasn't ready to like him; so instead of reacting, I simply turned and left.

Because it's harder to kill people you like if circumstances called for it.

CHAPTER TWELVE

Zephyr

THIS WAS SO COOL. I HAD MET THE GIRL OF MY DREAMS at a nightclub, and now we were going on an adventure. The other guys had tried to make it sound scary, but all I could think about was why on earth would anyone want to hurt Rowen? She was so cool, and the guys were like the big brothers I never got to have. I mean, they bickered and fought for Rowen's attention, but you could see they actually liked each other under it all.

I called my parents on the way to the airport and explained I'd met a girl and was going to go traveling with her. Turned out, they knew Rowen's parents. Didn't run in the same circles, though, which wasn't a surprise.

My parents were eco entrepreneurs who frequently donated large percentages of their profits to charity. Their actions had shocked the old money crowds, who were already inclined to dislike self-made millionaires. Especially when my dad was Korean and my mom was from Boston.

Racists, elitists, and sociopaths were the norm in the 'upper echelon' of society.

For my part, I was proud my parents gave a shit about humanity. Everything I heard about Rowen's family made me want to hug her and invite her to dinner so she could see that not all rich people were boring asses. Some were actually pretty cool.

Sullivan and Jett were arguing about something while we waited for our next flight, so I got to play cameraman for Rowen while she filmed her vlog update. She smiled warmly at the camera, and I noticed her lips were still pink from my kisses earlier.

"Hey, bestie babes! How have you gone with our clues so far? If you guessed Tonga, you were correct! What an amazing time I've had, but now we're on to our next destination." Her smile dropped for a second as she mentioned the country we definitely were not in, but a moment later, she was back in character.

"In the home of the hobbits, you can feel like a goddess after visiting this country's hot springs. And if you're needing sleep, there are plenty of sheep to count. Where in the world am I? I'll leave you to puzzle that one out, and in the meantime, remember, you only live once, so live chic!" She smiled and froze.

"Turn the camera off, idiot," Jett called from the seat he had taken.

Right. I pressed stop and handed her camera back.

"Why did you use the destination we're actually going to? I thought we agreed to do the one you were leaving," Sullivan asked with a scowl.

"It's a stopover, and we'll be there in five hours. It'll be fine. I don't like lying any more than I have to," Rowen said, glancing at the ceiling as our flight was called for boarding.

"I don't like it," Sullivan grumbled, pushing past Linden to be behind Rowen as we boarded.

There was something about her that drew people in, and I was sure the others felt it too. I didn't mind. As long as I got to be with her, I didn't care who else wanted to be too. It was up to her, after all, who she let in.

***

Auckland airport was amazing. Once we cleared customs, I took the opportunity to buy some duty-free clothing and change out of my clubbing outfit. Which was a relief, because even though it had great memories from the night before, it was kind of rank. I didn't want to make Rowen sit with someone who smelled.

"So why exactly are you tagging along on this trip, pup?" Sullivan asked, sliding into the egg-shaped seat beside me.

It was funny how all three of the guys had started calling me a puppy. Joke was on them; I loved dogs. I wasn't upset about the suspicion, either. It was awesome knowing there was a group of us that had her back.

I shrugged at the big guy, who was actually a marshmallow. No, I would not be saying that to his face. But I had heard him on the phone with his sister earlier, and I knew she was his original reason for not hurting Rowen.

"I decided she's my person. I'm going to stick with her as long as I can make her happy."

Sullivan grunted and shifted in his seat. It was easy to see he was too big for the thing, but he was in now. It was going to be hilarious seeing him get back out later.

"So that's it. One night with her and she's yours?"

I laughed. I couldn't help it, but he so didn't get it.

"Nah, man. I'm hers. If she has others, that's cool too. I just hope I get to stick around."

Sullivan glanced over at the girl in question where she lay with her head in Linden's lap. Jett shot covert glances at the pair from across the way, and I wondered if he or Sullivan had considered a girl with a heart that big had room for all of us.

"Are you telling me you would be okay with her cheating on you with one of us?"

"Cheating? No, that's not my deal, but a relationship is what you make it. I had these friends when I lived in Louisiana who were in a committed polyamorous relationship. Three guys and a girl, and I tell you, man, they had it good. They were a real family, you know? They treated her like a queen and each other like brothers. I think it would be awesome to be able to live like that."

I could tell I'd piqued the Irishman's curiosity. His egg chair almost toppled as he sat forward. Coughing to cover a laugh, I pulled out my cell to find a photo of the group I was talking about. Sullivan took the device and scowled at the screen.

"They look happy, but don't they get jealous? Who does she love most?"

"That's the point. There is no most. I mean, they bicker, sure, same as you and Jett. But they care about each other. And at the end of the day, isn't that the only thing that matters? You don't have to share the intimate time if you don't want to, but I have to tell you, it was smoking hot sharing her with Linden last night."

Linden had been in complete control, and I was man enough to admit that seeing her react to him had been a huge turn-on for me.

Sullivan's head whipped back toward Rowen and Linden a half second before his egg chair crumpled beneath him.

"Are you okay?" I asked in between laughter, holding my belly and trying to catch my breath while I helped him out of his plastic cage.

"Stop laughing, you little shite," he growled, but I saw the smile at the corner of his mouth even as he pulled his ass free of the wreckage.

"What happened?" Rowen asked, taking Sullivan by the arm with a look of concern.

His whole face softened, and his eyes dropped to where they were touching. I wondered if she knew, if anyone else had realized. We were already becoming a family. Even if we'd only known each other for a few days. Hours, in my case.

"Shoddy workmanship," Sullivan said with significantly less grump than a moment before.

"The chair was fine. Your ass was just too big for it," Jett said with a laugh, moving in next to Rowen.

Whatever Sullivan's reply would have been was cut off by our boarding announcement.

"You ready?" he asked Rowen instead.

"To lie again? I suppose I have to be, right?"

We all knew this part of her safety plan was her least favorite. She was a naturally honest person, and I could imagine it grated having to intentionally mislead people, but I also got why Sullivan and Jett insisted on it.

They were quite similar when I thought about it. Although they would probably kick my ass for saying it. They were protectors, and the idea they couldn't totally keep our girl safe was driving them crazy. So they decompressed by arguing with each other.

"I'm the cameraman," Jett rumbled, swiping the cell phone from Sullivan's hand. Rowen sighed and wiped her hands on her skirt.

"Okay, I'm ready," she said, nodding and flashing a smile.

I hated that smile. It wasn't real. I wanted to see the smile she wore when we were dancing again. There had been no sign of it since we showered and left our bungalow this morning, and I missed it already.

"All right. In three. Two." Jett held up a finger, then pointed at Rowen as he hit record. I smothered a snort at the blatant attempt to show how good of a cameraman he could be.

"Hey, bestie babes! What a whirlwind visit this has been! Did you guess we'd made it all the way to the other side of the world? New Zealand! What a magical place this is. Even the airport has amazing works of art. Our next stop is only a short flight away, so are you ready for the clue? It's stinking hot on this jungle-filled island, but at least the locals are cute, even if they're covered in orange hair! Good luck, because this is a hard one. Remember, you only live once, so live chic." She blew a kiss, and Jett's ears went red as he stopped the recording and handed her cell over with a rare smile.

"You really don't think it'd work?" I muttered smugly as I followed Sullivan into line for our flight.

"You're getting a whack on the nose with a rolled-up newspaper in a moment," he deadpanned.

Who knew he was funny?

Boarding and getting seated was uneventful. Jett scored the seat next to Rowen, but I figured it was fair. I'd gotten the bed the night before, and it was only a three-hour flight. I couldn't wait to get to our next stop. It was a bucket list country for me.

I was reading an article about places to visit when Sullivan leaned over the back of our seat to slap Linden awake.

"We've got a problem. Go swap seats with Jett. I need to talk to him."

I opened my mouth to volunteer and caught a slap to my head.

"You can't go anywhere near her. You're the only one of us my bosses don't know about."

Well, crud. He had a point.

Linden shuffled out of our row, and a moment later, Jett came grumbling through. "What do you want?"

"Blade's on this flight. He knows we're here, so we need an airtight plan to get her out safely."

"How do you think he found us?" I asked.

"How do you think? The fucking vlog. I told her not to tell the truth," Sullivan hissed, spittle flying from his mouth in his frustration. It was kinda gross, but he was my homie, so we were good.

"So what's the plan here? You know the guy, right? Does he have any weaknesses? We can't do much to him on the flight, but we could jump him once we land," Jett said thoughtfully.

"We need to get her clear safely first. Blade is an idiot, but he's deadly. Has a hard-on for weapons. Especially knives, if you hadn't guessed from the stupid name."

Jett huffed. "Okay. So decoy might be easiest. We need someone to run interference while we get Rowen clear."

Sullivan nodded. "Right. Someone who has no known association with Rowen or any of us."

"Who we can trust to do exactly as they're told. Get in, get out, and not try to play the hero."

I nodded along with their plan, feeling really happy to be watching them work their magic. They were an excellent team when they were on the same wavelength.

The sudden quiet caught my attention, and when I looked up, their eyes were on me.

"What? Me?" I didn't think they would care that I was more cheerleader than international man of mystery or whatever, but if it kept Rowen safe?

I was all in.

CHAPTER THIRTEEN

Sullivan

Fucking Blade. He was like the case of herpes he'd contracted in an unlicensed brothel after the first job we worked together. Relentless, irritating as fuck, and apparently my fucking problem. For the record, I'd had nothing to do with the visit, but every job we had worked since, he'd found a way to bring the shit up. Asshole.

Once the plan was in place, I kicked Linden to my seat so I could sit with Rowen under the guise of briefing her on the situation.

"Are you okay? Why does everyone keep shuffling?" Rowen asked as I dropped into the seat beside her.

"Slight complication. Nothing to worry about, but I need you to be aware. Blade is on this flight."

She gasped and tried to look around for the man in question.

Bracing a hand on her shoulder, I kept her in her seat. "Don't draw attention to yourself. We're going to get you out, okay? You're safe with us. Puppy is going to play decoy. Linden will escort you out of the building and straight to a cab as soon as we land. He'll pay off customs and get you the fuck to safety while Jett and I cover your escape. No matter what happens, you keep going. Do you understand?"

"But I don't—"

"Sorry, *a pheata*, this isn't a discussion. Jett and I, we're trained for this shit. We will keep you safe. If you're around, you put us in danger because you divide our attention. You're too important to lose, okay?"

She opened her mouth and closed it again. I really hoped she didn't ask any questions about what I'd just said, because I had no fucking clue where it had come from. It was true, though. Above and beyond the fact she made my baby sister smile, she deserved far better than whatever this shit was she had become tangled up in.

"I'm also going to need your hacker friend's number. There's some shit in my files that I need her to crack so we can figure out who the hell started all this."

She nodded, eyes wide and a little too glassy for my liking.

"You'll be fine," I repeated, as much for my benefit as for hers.

"Why are you doing all this for me?" she asked, avoiding eye contact as she scribbled Makenna's name and number on a scrap of paper for me. "All of you. Why haven't you just walked away? I keep waiting for you all to realize I'm not worth the trouble and leave. Everyone leaves. So why haven't you?"

Her eyes caught and held mine as I took the paper from her. Would the truth scare her? Maybe it would give her the security she seemed to need.

"None of us are going anywhere. I promise you. We are not going to leave you to face this alone."

"But why? I don't understand—"

I lost my mind. All rational thought fled, and I became a creature of instinct. That was the only excuse I had for why I reached across the space between us and pulled her into a soul-searing kiss.

Fuck Blade, fuck my ex-employers, fuck whoever thought they could take this girl from me.

There was a moment when I thought she would resist. I had taken her by surprise—had taken myself by surprise—and I knew I should give her space. But then her fingertips brushed my jaw and I was lost all over again.

Through a haze of lust, the ping of the seatbelt sign reminded me we were far from alone, and there was work to be done to ensure our first kiss wasn't also our last.

"No matter what, stay with Linden and get away as quickly as possible, okay?"

At her nod, I pecked a last kiss to her pink lips and headed back to my original seat for landing. Linden raised an unimpressed eyebrow as we passed in the aisle.

I shook my head. "Later."

Sliding into my seat, I reached around to the row ahead of me and knocked Zephyr over the head. "You may just be on to something, pup. Now let's see if we survive the next twenty-four hours."

He smirked back at me while Jett scowled at the both of us, clearly unhappy he wasn't in on the joke.

Instead of clueing him in, I asked, "We ready to go?"

Both men nodded as the plane descended toward the runway.

Showtime.

Blade was in the far back corner of the plane, and while I knew he would have seen us moving around—and probably the kiss, I belatedly realized—he wouldn't be able to see the Korean-American human embodiment of a golden retriever we had picked up at our last stop.

Zephyr was our wild card, and the only member of our group who hadn't yet been identified in the mission paperwork. I would never admit it aloud, but the kid was growing on me. Fucking ball of sunshine that he was. Ray would like him.

I needed to check in on Ray and Mam, but it would have to wait an hour or two. As far as my ex-employers knew, I was an orphan who had grown up around the IRA members hidden in our community. Partially true. Those scary old fucks kept everyone in our village on the straight and narrow. No one wanted to be taken out to The Bog and have their kneecaps threatened with a shotgun.

Mam and Rayleigh were ghosts to anyone outside of our village, and I wanted to ensure it stayed that way.

The wheels touched down, and I held my breath as the airplane took an eternity to taxi down the runway toward the terminal.

No delays, I thought. *We need this to go smoothly*.

We rolled to a smooth stop, and I allowed myself to relax the slightest bit as the seatbelt sign extinguished and Linden leaped to his feet, pulling Rowen with him. Leaving the carry-on luggage for us to deal with, he pushed toward the front, past the protesting flight attendants. His deep voice drifted back to us as he told a steward he was a doctor and his patient couldn't be crushed in the departing crowd.

Blade was also on his feet, pushing through passengers who had followed Linden's example and filed into the aisle.

"Puppy, you're up," I muttered, sliding out of my seat and retrieving everyone's carry-ons before pushing toward the front of the plane.

The doors had yet to be opened, and I was feeling somewhat like a sardine. As stupid as it sounded, I was too tall for this shit.

"Oh! Sorry, I didn't see you there. Wow, is that a Henley shirt? I think I have the same one."

I couldn't help but smirk as Zephyr made contact with Blade. The bubbly voice sounded so innocent. I may have underestimated the kid. *He was smarter than I gave him credit for, and thank God for it,* I thought as he dragged other passengers into a conversation about a black t-shirt.

As the doors opened and passengers started to disembark, a heavy hand on my shoulder was my signal Jett had made it past Zephyr and was ready to proceed.

"I hope the kid knows what he's doing," Jett whispered as we smiled politely at the stewards.

A scream echoed over the heads of the passengers, and I felt my stomach drop as the words "stabbed", "bleeding", and "doctor" were repeated by many voices.

"Keep going. The kid will be all right. If we go back, Blade will finish the job." Fuck. I hated myself for saying it, and the look on Jett's face told me he felt the same.

As soon as Rowen was clear, we'd send Linden to find Zephyr while we neutralized Blade. No restraints this time. I was going to use his own knife on him. And if the kid was dead? Shit was going to get messy.

Passing through customs was a pain in the ass, but I was happy to see Linden and Rowen were absent. Fucking doctor powers were scary sometimes. Blade was in a separate line that appeared to be moving slower than ours, small blessing that was.

I hadn't seen the kid yet. It hadn't escaped me that Jett kept looking for him too. I realized I had held out hope that someone else had been on the receiving end of the knife. Shit. If he didn't make it, I was never going to forgive myself.

As I handed my customs declaration over, my cell chimed with an incoming message.

"She's clear," Jett muttered, looking up from where the same message had come through on his cell.

"Thank fuck."

"Business or pleasure?" the customs officer asked, typing on her computer and taking far too long to let us get on with it.

"Ahh... it's... been on my bucket list for years. Happy to finally get here," I said with a strained smile, thinking of how excited Zephyr had been to come here.

The woman smiled warmly and returned our passports, waving us through. "Well, enjoy your stay."

We both nodded and hustled to the baggage claim, positioning ourselves so we could see Blade when he came through.

"I don't like this. How was he not arrested for publicly stabbing someone in the middle of a crowded airplane?" Jett looked, for all the world, like he was bored out of his mind while waiting for our bags, but I saw the way his eyes darted around, studying every face.

I'd had the same thought. Whoever was funding this hunt had deep pockets and friends in high places.

Taking advantage of our waiting time, I pulled out my cell and made two calls. The first was to Linden who listened calmly to what had happened and promised he would follow it up. I was thankful he didn't let Rowen know what was happening. She would only blame herself.

I called the second number and listened to it ring five times before a slightly hostile voice came through the speaker. "Who is this, and how did you get this number?"

"I'm a friend of Rowen's. Look—"

"Sullivan. Nice to meet you. Why am I talking to you and not Rowen?" She'd done her homework, clearly. Although, how difficult could it be to pick the only Irishman from the group by voice alone?

"She's safe for now, but we have problems. Rowen said you're a good hacker—"

"I'm the best, but go on."

"Okay, well, I'm hoping you're the person for the job, then. There are hidden files on an encrypted network that I can't crack."

The crinkle of foil broke the silence on the other end. "What's the IP address on your computer?"

"I have..."

"Doesn't matter. Give me the address of the server you last used, and I'll track it back to the program."

I promised to text the address to her and was ready to end the call when she cleared her throat.

"I don't know what the heck is going on yet, but it's serious, Sullivan. There was a virus in the email that started all of this. It was programmed to take out all the electricity in the building. I'm talking security, elevators, locks, everything. She isn't taking this seriously, and I do not want my friend dead. Whoever is after her, get rid of them and bring her home safe."

"I plan to."

I ended the call, more worried than ever. At the same moment, Blade came into view. Without stopping for luggage, he headed straight for the exit. Of course, his luggage wouldn't pass any kind of security check. With a hand to the chest, I stopped Jett from pursuing. "Get the bags, then catch up. I've got this."

"You haven't got shit. You don't go in alone."

I grinned, injecting every ounce of nastiness I possessed into the expression. "You're unarmed. I'm not. It's time to neutralize the threat once and for all. Just make sure you're there in time for cleanup."

"I thought you hadn't killed before," he asked, lowering his voice as people jostled by us.

"First time for everything, and he kicked my puppy."

Jett barked a surprised laugh and pointed a sharp finger at me. "This doesn't mean I like you, but don't get killed. Try to leave some fun for me."

I jogged toward the exit with a genuine smile on my face.

There was no better way to bond than over the demise of someone who was pissing on everyone's parade.

CHAPTER FOURTEEN

Rowen

SOMETHING WAS DEFINITELY WRONG. LINDEN ENDED his call with a calm mask in place that honestly made him look a little scary.

"Everything okay?" I asked hesitantly.

He glanced over as though having forgotten I was in the cab with him. "Hmm? Yes, fine. Once we get to the hotel, I want you to stay put. I have something I need to take care of, and you can't be out alone at the moment."

"Are the others okay? Was that Sullivan?"

He hummed a noise that could have been a yes or a stop talking and frowned down at his cell as he tapped furiously at the screen.

"Linden?"

When he didn't answer, I curled up against the door of the cab and watched the scenery go by.

I had finally become too much of a hassle. I didn't blame them, but it hurt more than expected. The cab turned, and the buildings gave way to water.

The Harbour City, Sydney. I wished I could see the Opera House from where we were. I wanted to run up the stairs and touch those white sails, but I caught a glimpse or two of the famous bridge as we wound through the streets toward Darling Harbour.

At our hotel, we wasted no time checking in and heading straight up to the penthouse apartment we were supposed to be staying in together. The moment we arrived, Linden issued orders to stay inside, away from the windows, and not to answer the door for anyone. And then he was gone, leaving me entirely alone.

I had spent the majority of my life in my own company, and had, for the most part, vastly preferred it to the alternative of old rich men, hoping to acquire a side piece who was well connected, or, even worse, my parents.

Speaking of my parents. I knew I should call them and at least let them know I was on the other side of the world with a group of strange men who were protecting me from someone who was trying to kill me. My side twinged, and I tucked myself under the blankets. Or maybe I could wait until tomorrow.

***

My next conscious thought was that I was starving. I rolled carefully onto my side to check the time and did a double take when it registered I had slept for eleven hours.

Eleven hours and there wasn't a single notification on my cell. Where had the guys gone? I clicked on to my vlog and smiled at the hundreds of replies my recent video had garnered. Guesses ranged from Papua New Guinea to... Scotland? There weren't any jungles in Scotland.

I found myself grinning at regular commenters who cheered me on, telling me to 'stick it to the scammers.' It wasn't as funny now that I knew the threat was real.

I had a quick shower, reluctantly pulling my travel clothes back on once I remembered my bags were all... somewhere.

Sullivan had sworn he would come for me. But he had also tried to abduct me not that long ago. Jett had already tolerated me for the longest. What if he'd dealt with Blade and decided to go and give Kylie another chance?

I thought about the guys one at a time and found it too easy to believe they might have found a better offer. After all, I was practically a stranger to them even if I was, maybe, possibly falling for each and every one of them. Who did that? Was I so selfish that I wanted to keep all four of them to myself? So arrogant to think they might want to?

My thoughts spiraled into the darkness in a way that was both familiar and disappointing. I had gone through a lot of therapy to try to stop this exact thing.

"What's one thing you can do to prove your thoughts wrong?" I asked myself out loud, pretending my old therapist was in the room with me.

I looked at my cell. It felt like an intrusion, but I reminded myself that it was purely my negative thoughts talking.

"Reach out," I said, resolutely hitting call on Zephyr's number.

Voicemail kicked in without it ringing. Linden's cell number did the same. Sullivan. I knew his cell was on. He had been coordinating everything. Surely. The call rang once, twice... On the sixth ring, the call dumped to voicemail.

Tears welled in my eyes.

"Jett." Surely, he would answer. He had been with me the longest. He promised he would be, as long as I wanted him here.

And I really wanted him here. My heart thudded painfully in my chest as I pulled up his number and hit send on the call. It rang twice, and I felt light-headed as the call connected.

"Hello, who's this?" a light, nasally Australian accent demanded.

The voice was male, but wrong. It wasn't Jett, and I was officially out of people to call. Without answering, I disconnected the line and crawled back to the center of the bed.

I wasn't hungry anymore.

CHAPTER FIFTEEN

Jett

"I CAN'T BELIEVE YOU LOST HIM," I GROUSED AS Sullivan hacked the public library computer we had managed to nab.

"I didn't lose him. Our cab driver was incompetent. We'll be back on track as soon as I can log in. Ah, see? Easy."

I didn't know what we were looking at. After following Blade out of the airport, we had jumped into a cab behind him and promptly lost the bastard in Sydney's shitty traffic. Our driver hadn't taken kindly to the orders to follow another car, and unfortunately, neither of us had the kind of money to throw around that the others did, so our broke asses were kicked out when we couldn't identify a destination.

We walked for a few miles until we found a library, where we were currently breaking library policy and using their internet facilities to commit a crime.

"Okay, good news is he's nowhere near our hotel," Sullivan concluded, sitting back in his seat.

"Right, so what's the bad news?" I asked, reaching into my pocket for my cell.

It had been a while since we checked in on Rowen. Coming up empty, I checked each of my pockets in turn.

"Fuck."

A woman bending over a small boy on the next station glared at me before turning back to the game on the screen. Oops.

"I lost my fucking phone," I growled, earning myself a second disapproving look.

"Well then, we have more bad news. We need to get another cab and head into the city. Blade is in Kings Cross, which, if my research is correct, means we're going to find him in a fucking brothel."

The woman beside us had gone an interesting shade of purple as she continued to glare.

Before I could utter a word, Sullivan glanced over casually with a wicked grin. "You know, it's rude to eavesdrop. What kind of a lesson are you teaching the little one? Tsk."

Fuck it. I was ready to admit I liked the giant leprechaun. He was an artist at pissing people off, and I had to admire his work.

"Remind me to bring you next time I have to see my family. I'm setting you loose on my ex," I said as he shut down his workstation, blowing a kiss to the bitch next door as we left.

"With pleasure. It's not work when you enjoy what you do."

This guy. I barked a laugh and slapped him on the back as we made our way back out into the city to hail another cab.

***

"This doesn't seem as good an idea as it did an hour ago," I admitted, staring up at a neon sign advertising Coca-Cola across the road from where we'd left our cab, giving the driver a hefty tip to deliver our luggage to our hotel.

"It'll be fine. I've taken a person or two from here in the past. It's easy."

I squinted up at him, unsure if he was serious. He shrugged. "Bounty hunting is a good job for jet setting. Seen the world a few times over. I'm also good at spotting a man in a crowd. Now come on."

We wandered down the main drag past brightly lit signs offering services and shows.

"I feel dirty just walking down this street," I admitted, walking a wide berth around a man in rags ranting loudly about shoes. The guy looked high as a kite and I felt sorry for him as a group of teens stopped to jeer at him.

"What kind of soldier are you? Most of the blokes I've met with your background would feel right at home here. There's even a Navy base at the bottom of the hill if you need a military fix."

I snorted. "This is the first time I've been single in over a decade. I may be one of the boys, but I'm no cheat."

Sullivan was quiet for a few moments. I surveyed our surroundings, hoping for a glimpse of the dark-haired man I remembered from the luau.

"Did Zephyr get a chance to talk to you about his theory?"

"No. What theory?" I couldn't imagine what the puppy could have said that would make Sullivan think so hard on it, but clearly something was up.

"He said he doesn't think Rowen should have to choose. Between us, I mean."

"Why would she be choosing between us? Nothing's going on." I didn't know why I denied how I felt, but clearly, Sullivan wasn't buying my shit.

"He thinks we could all share. Be like... a family, or something. I dunno, he said it better. It's stupid. Forget it. I shouldn't have brought it up." Sullivan scrubbed at the back of his neck and increased his pace, but it didn't stop me from seeing his ears flame red.

Every part of me wanted to deny it. To let him go and pretend we hadn't started this conversation. But that didn't do anything but put up barriers when we needed to work together.

"Kylie used to read books like that. It's called a reverse harem," I said to his back.

"A reverse what?"

I chuckled. "Yeah, I know. She talked about them a lot. Come to think of it, maybe she hoped she could build one with Felix and me."

"That's kinda messed up, man," Sullivan said, falling back beside me again as we reached a bend in the road. Across from us was a large fountain, and behind it, a police station. Something to watch out for if we were serious about ridding ourselves of Blade as a threat permanently.

"Yeah, well. Felix is a dick who would never share. And Kylie... well... but Rowen?"

"I know. I've been thinking the same. I guess you blokes are all right, even if the puppy needs a collar."

We sobered at the reminder that Zephyr may not be fine.

"Fuck, I hope Linden found him," I breathed.

Sullivan nodded.

Could I share Rowen with these guys? Hell, it almost felt like we already were. She had a way of checking in on each of us. Knowing when we needed a bit more attention than the rest. She really was perfect for us. All of us.

Shit. I was considering it. More than considering. It sounded like a good idea.

By unspoken agreement, we turned and headed back up the hill at a stroll. Just two guys perusing their options in a not-so-great part of town. Girls called to us across the road, trying to coax us into their establishments, but we walked on until Sullivan pulled us down a side street.

"I just need to check the camera positioning." We continued at the same pace, Sullivan discreetly showing me each of the CCTV cameras positioned around the streets for public safety.

"Here." He decided a short time later. Hidden by the back of a food establishment that seemed to be closed, the back wall of the courtyard was crumbling in places, allowing access while also creating a blind spot in surveillance. Perfect for our needs.

"Not ideal for avoiding detection on the way in or out, but we'll make it work. All right. Stay here and wait for the signal."

I grabbed his arm as he turned to leave. "What the fuck do you think you're doing? We aren't separating. We do this as a team."

"We are. You're the ambush. I'm the bait."

He was insane. I remembered the flag on his profile. Kill on sight. The idiot was going to make himself a visible target and lure Blade back here. I wanted to fight it. It was stupid, and he was going to get himself killed, but I also had nothing better. Beggars/choosers and all that. He knew the moment I came to the same conclusion as he had and grinned madly before taking off into the growing darkness.

This was such a bad idea.

I couldn't have said how long I waited for Sullivan to return. Enough times that I had mentally related the story of his stupid demise to Rowen a couple dozen times and the light had completely faded from the sky.

This felt too much like being on deployment. Holed up in some nowhere town, waiting for the enemy to turn up, and hoping when the dust cleared, it wasn't your body on the ground. And if it was, hoping it wasn't the permanent kind of injury.

My left calf ached with remembered pain from the shrapnel wound I'd received last time I saw action. It wasn't the first injury I'd sustained in service, but it was the most fresh in my mind. Especially when I'd taken it while trying to save a dead man. I shook my head hard and looked up at the few stars I could see through the city's light haze. These were the nights I missed home.

The scuff of a boot set my heart pounding as adrenaline flooded my system. *Calm*, I ordered myself. My ears rang as I strained to hear the next movement. It might not be them. It might not be time.

A lyrical voice began to sing a bawdy song that I vaguely remembered hearing from the last Irishman I had met. Sullivan. I held my position. They would come to me.

"What's wrong wi' ye, Blade? Ye don't want to play?" The words were slurred and accompanied by a shuffling step.

Smart. A stumbling, drunk target, alone in the back alley of a foreign country, seemed like an easy mark.

Starting up the tune again, Sullivan's stumbling step shuffled toward the shadow I hid in. Between one breath and the next, he flipped over the crumbling wall in a sprawl that I hoped to hell had been convincing.

"Fuck," he mumbled, scraping around and moving into the one small patch of light in the courtyard.

Jesus. No way was Blade going to buy this.

Sullivan's eyes flashed in warning a second before a shadow appeared over the wall.

I didn't think. Hesitation got you killed when you were playing with life or death. Sullivan rolled out of the light as I grabbed the back of Blade's head and introduced his face to the crumbling wall. Hauling him over the cracked brickwork, I threw him into the middle of the courtyard.

Bastard was faster than I gave him credit for. Rolling into a crouch, he fired two rounds in my direction before turning to seek Sullivan out in the shadows.

"Come on, Irish. Come and play," he growled.

I had no clue how such a large man hid so well, but I was as shocked as Blade when Sullivan lunged out of the shadows. They hit the ground in a heap. Fucking Sullivan insisting on darkness. I couldn't see a thing.

There was the slap of flesh on flesh, and the crunch of something that probably shouldn't crunch. I crouched, waiting for any sign of how I could help. Fuck, I felt completely useless here.

The next sound froze the heart in my chest. Two small whispers of air and I knew someone had been shot.

Tell me Sullivan got the gun, I prayed desperately as I prepared to... what? A shadow rose from the ground, but it was too small. Bulkier than it should have been. Blade.

Easing along the perimeter of the small courtyard, I searched around me for a brick to distract the fucker. My fingers closed around a solid chunk, and as the bastard stepped into the sliver of light, I threw. The block hit him in the temple as I followed close behind, disarming him and throwing the gun into the shadows, well out of reach. I needed to finish this quickly.

Hold on, Sullivan.

A fist to the face pulled my attention back to the moment as I blinked the pain out of my eyes and sidestepped the next punch. Jab, cross, block. I had fought competitively for years in the military, and I knew this guy was not to be underestimated.

Blocking a high hit, Blade left his side exposed. I took the opening, stepped inside his guard, and found myself flat on my back with a knife to my throat.

Blade tutted. "I thought you were going to make it difficult. Shame you won't be around to see what happens next to your girlfriend."

I bucked beneath him, ignoring the bite of the steel at my throat. Fuck him, he wasn't going to...

Bang.

Blade slumped onto my chest like a puppet with his strings cut. Come to think of it, that's exactly what he was.

I rolled the body off me, wiping blood and brain matter from my lips with the back of an arm.

"You couldn't have found a better angle?" I groused, pushing up to my feet and shuffling into the darkness toward my companion. A wheezing chuckle helped me find the big guy, laid out in a corner and doing a good impression of a fountain.

"Shot to the head means he won't get back up. I saved your life. You're welcome." His voice was thin, and the truth hit me that I may still lose him.

"You did this on purpose. Making me do all the work to save your ass. You could have just asked for a piggy-back. I mean, I would have said no, but still... don't you think this is a bit much?"

Sullivan huffed a laugh that turned into a groan as I heaved him into a fireman's carry.

"How you doing, buddy? You still with me?"

No reply, but I could feel his heart beating against my back. So with a quick thanks to whoever was listening that we had passed a hospital not far from the Coca-Cola sign that was almost overhead, I hustled toward the nearest source of medical assistance.

CHAPTER SIXTEEN

Linden

AFTER HOURS OF CAREFUL INQUIRY, THREATS, AND blatant bribery, I finally found out Zephyr was in surgery in Saint Vincent's hospital. Problem was, that was as far as I made it.

Seated in the waiting area, I glared daggers at the nurse who had so far refused to be of assistance in the provision of any information pertaining to Zephyr's condition. "In surgery" was all she would say, before asking for his next of kin.

I had considered tracking down his parents, but found myself unable to leave until I knew for sure he was safely out of surgery at the least. My cell was switched off, as per hospital policy, but I couldn't help playing with it, hoping Rowen was all right. Hoping the others had taken care of Blade and made it back to her. That we could all pull through and keep going without anyone else coming to harm.

Time held no meaning in the artificial lighting of the hospital, but I thought a shift of nurses may have changed? New faces were passing by, looking slightly less weary than the last.

The doors at the end of the corridor burst open, and Jett was there. Bloody from head to foot. I surged out of my chair in a panic as every nurse in sight headed for the big blonde who looked like death incarnate.

"What...?" I asked as he spotted me.

"Sullivan. How's Zephyr? Where's Rowen?"

"Is he...?"

"I don't know. Rowen?"

"I left her at the hotel. I thought you guys were done hours ago. What happened?"

Jett waved the fussing nurses away with a bloody hand.

"Complications. Are you telling me she's been alone this whole time?"

Complications. Shit. If I had been the weak link that compromised Rowen's safety, I would never forgive myself. The floors squeaked under the tennis shoes of hospital staff as they moved between rooms on the ward, and I took a moment to marvel at how the sound came as a comfort. The familiar in a terribly unfamiliar situation.

"Have you spoken to her?" I asked, waving him into a seat before resuming my own.

"I lost my cell. You?"

I pointed at a sign nearby that reminded patrons to switch their cells off while in the hospital.

"Zephyr's in surgery. They won't tell me any more than that because I'm not family."

Jett nodded silently, and for a while, we just sat.

People passed by. Visitors. Staff. Most eyed Jett carefully, as though they may be the next thing on his agenda. He did a remarkable job of acting oblivious to it all.

I had resorted to flipping through a women's magazine full of health tips when Jett slapped his thighs, stood, and headed for the nurse's station.

"Jett...?" I asked carefully.

It had been a long night, and he looked like he was capable of anything. Ignoring me, he ambled over to the night nurse and hung half over the desk.

"Hi," he said, flashing a winning grin that may have lost some of its appeal as dried blood flaked off his skin and onto the papers she had been working on.

"Can I help you?" Whatever he had planned, this was not going to work.

"I have two friends in here who were in a bad way when they came in. I would love to know exactly how both are doing. Thank you."

"No."

Jett sucked in a breath as though disappointed and knocked his hand on the desk. "You see now, I'm going to have to insist. Both of those men are under the United States government jurisdiction. They were injured in the line of duty, and I have a responsibility to their families to report up-to-date information on their injury status."

"No. When the patients are conscious and able to provide verbal consent, then you will be admitted to see them. If they are stable."

Jett cursed and returned to his seat. "Can't you just bribe her or something?"

I shrugged. "I tried. Almost got kicked out. At this point, I figured I could wait for the next shift and hope for better luck, or sit here until they're so sick of me they give me information to get me out."

He nodded.

"You really should go to the hotel for a shower, though. I think I can see a piece of bone matter in your hair."

"Probably," he said with a shrug.

CHAPTER SEVENTEEN

Rowen

THE CLICK OF THE LOCK DISENGAGING ON THE HOTEL room door was a shock after so long in silence. I leaped to my feet, equal parts excited and terrified. Was it the guys? Someone else? I moved on careful feet toward the entryway and screamed at the blood-covered man standing in the doorway.

He yelled something that could have been "It's me," or "Kimchi" or maybe "Kill bees," I couldn't be sure, but self-protection mode was activated and I flailed around for a weapon.

The food fermenting bee murderer dodged as I threw anything I could get my hands on. First my slippers, one after the other, then a book, a magazine that fluttered off without getting anywhere near my target, then the phone receiver—which was still attached to the phone, unfortunately.

As I reached across the bed toward the closest pillow, the man caught my hand and spun me toward him.

"Rowen. It's me. Jett."

His words broke through the panic a moment later, and I melted into his arms. "I thought you'd left. I thought you were done with me. Where have you all been?" Tears burned my eyes and spilled down my cheeks as the realization that Jett had returned hit full force.

"I told you before. You have me for as long as you want me. The others feel the same way, too."

"How could you possibly know that?" I asked, sniffing away my tears.

Jett shuffled his feet.

"Look, could we talk about this when I'm not wearing a dead man's blood?"

I looked down at his shirt and felt the panic rising again. "Sullivan."

Jett shook his head and pulled me into a hug, blood or no blood.

"You're going to need a shower, too, at this rate," Jett mumbled.

I poked him and scowled.

"Tell me," I said.

"Blade stabbed Zephyr as we were leaving the plane. Linden went to find out where he had been transported to. We'd just gotten the report he was out of surgery when I left. Sullivan was shot. It was pure coincidence we ended up in the same hospital. Linden's still there, trying to get some information. Blade is dead. It's been a really long night, but if you feel up for it, after I grab a shower, we can get breakfast and head back. See if there's any more news."

That... was a lot. They'd all been risking their lives to keep me safe while I assumed they had left me. I felt like an idiot.

While I sat and processed the new information, Jett nodded gruffly and moved into the bathroom.

A rush of water broke the silence of the room, and I shamelessly edged toward the bathroom door. It stood ajar. A small gap, just wide enough to show him slowly remove the soiled clothing he had been wearing since Auckland.

It felt explicit, watching the muscles in his back flex in the light as he threw his shirt to the side and worked on the buckle of his pants. His shoes thumped into the wall one at a time as he kicked his feet free, then shucked his pants and boxers in a single move. I told myself to look away, but stood mesmerized as his golden skin was exposed. Scars that I had missed when we went swimming in Hawaii criss-crossed one calf, and I felt the urge to trace them. To learn their story.

"You can join me if you like."

I snapped my eyes up to meet his intense gaze in the mirror. *Busted.*

Moving slowly, I approached the bathroom with a caution borne from the knowledge that this was a tipping point. With Linden and Zephyr, I had told myself it was a one-time thing. We were having fun and it wouldn't hurt when they left because I wouldn't let them in far enough to hurt.

But we were past that now. They were all in, and I knew I was too.

Pulling my tank top over my head, I allowed myself to enjoy the heat in Jett's eyes. They worshipped me, the weight almost heavy as a caress as they took in the skin I exposed.

"I think I fell in love with you the moment you saved me from eating tomatoes," Jett said, taking a small step toward me.

"Love?" I asked. "You were still in a relationship with Kylie on that flight."

He shrugged. "You know how that ended, and besides, a woman who will straddle a stranger to avoid kneeing him in the balls is a keeper."

I chuckled, but then sobered. "What about the others? I'll be honest, you aren't the only one I care about."

I was a horrible person. I couldn't just be happy with one? What was wrong with me?

"I think it's called a reverse harem? But that's something you might have to take up with them," Jett said, then stepped past me into the water. "Give me a second to wash the blood away. I've waited too long for this to ruin it with a little murder."

I choked on a laugh. "We've known each other for what? A week?"

He grinned. "I've been waiting for you my whole life, Rowen. I just didn't know it."

I had expected sex when I stepped into the shower, but Jett told me we could wait until we knew exactly where my relationship with everyone stood. Considering how badly my side was aching after my mistreatment of it over the last few days, I was thankful for the reprieve.

Jett washed my hair, massaging my scalp in a way that sent tingles racing along my skin. He soaped me up carefully until I was a hot, panting mess, and then he dropped to his knees and brought me to a gentle climax on his tongue. When we stepped out of the shower, I was spotless, sated, and ready for another nap, but we had places to be. Jett called the front desk, and they confirmed our luggage had arrived. Once we had slipped into fresh clothing, it was time to find out the fate of the other men I had fallen for.

CHAPTER EIGHTEEN

Zephyr

WAKING UP IN A HOSPITAL WAS AN UNEXPECTED inconvenience. The bed was kind of uncomfortable and there was a needle in my arm. I hated needles. Even worse, I was alone and had no memory of how I'd come to be here. Above my bed sat a controller to call the nurse. That could work. Maybe they knew what happened.

I hoped Rowen had gotten away okay.

The last thing I remembered was Sullivan's plan to keep Rowen safe from that Blade guy. I was slowing him down like a good distraction should and then... I put a hand to my ribs and noticed they had been strapped tightly.

Huh. Had he stabbed me? That wasn't cool, but it looked like I was fine now, so suck it, dude. I pushed the button and grinned pleasantly at the nurse who bustled in, looking harried, ten minutes later.

"Can I see my friends?" I asked in my best 'please help me' voice.

The nurse grunted and walked out, which was kind of rude, but in the next minute, Linden strode through the door.

"Thank fuck you're okay, pup. You gave us a scare for a minute there."

I thought he was going to come in for a hug—which would have been pretty great, I liked hugs—but he moved straight to my chart and started reading.

"So what's the diagnosis, doc? Am I going to make it?" I asked, grinning.

"The diagnosis is you're the luckiest son of a bitch around. Second only maybe to him." Linden pulled back the curtain between my bed and the next to show Sullivan sleeping peacefully.

"When did he get here?" I asked, bewildered.

I didn't like seeing Sullivan that way. It made him seem too... I dunno... human?

"He's fine, kid. We're all fine," Linden assured me, sitting on the edge of my bed.

"Rowen?"

"On her way with Jett. They're bringing breakfast."

I nodded, settling back into my mattress to wait for my girl to show.

It didn't take long, but Sullivan was conscious and griping by the time she breezed through the door looking radiant.

Jett strolled in behind her, looking more relaxed than I'd seen him in a while. *Good for them.* After having some kind of silent eye conversation with Sullivan over Rowen's head, Jett nodded and came to sit with me.

"So," he said, trying to look like he wasn't completely uncomfortable as he cast a quick glance at where Rowen was fussing over Sullivan's strapped shoulder. We were going to run out of luck with gunshot wounds one of these days, but I was sure glad our good fortune had held so far. Jett cleared his throat. "Ah... Sullivan told me a bit about your theory, about Rowen. About how we could be a harem? If... fuck. It sounds stupid even asking. Forget it."

Hot damn, they were on board! This was awesome! I could introduce them all to my family and we could all have Christmas together. Maybe we could get a house with a huge-ass bed.

"I can already tell you're getting carried away with this idea. How about we let Rowen decide first, yeah?" Jett was doing some Jedi mind thing. He could totally tell what I was thinking. Cool.

At her name, Rowen turned, questions written all over her face.

"Can we all be your harem?" I asked.

Jett slapped me over the head as Sullivan wheezed out a laugh. "Smooth, puppy. We really need to teach you about tact."

I shrugged, unrepentant. This was going to be awesome.

"We could take things slowly. See what comes of each of the relationships. No pressure if it doesn't work, but we know you don't want to choose, and we all make a pretty good team." I was pretty sure that was the most words I had ever heard Jett say at one time.

Rowen looked from one face to the next, and I knew what she saw. We were all in, one hundred percent. Linden was last, and he nodded kindly to her.

"I think you're stuck with us."

Rowen grinned.

"Sounds like a plan."

"Excellent," Sullivan said, attempting to pull himself upright before lying back with a groan. "Much as I'd like to consummate our new arrangement the old-fashioned way, I might have to settle for a kiss." He looped a finger through Rowen's belt, drawing her toward the bed with a glint in his eye that told the males in the room he didn't have a liplock in mind. She bent over his bed, giving me an excellent view of her ass, cupped perfectly in her jeans. "Wrong lips, *a pheata*," he murmured, and I was man enough to admit I felt an echo of the shiver that rippled down her spine. Damn, these guys were good. I'd be able to learn lots about pleasing our woman from them.

Jett snorted. "Am I the only one who isn't an exhibitionist here?"

I laughed. "Lucky you like to watch, huh?"

Jett's pale skin flushed, and he retreated from the room with a murmured excuse about keeping nurses and doctors out. I didn't miss the way Rowen's eyes tracked him out the door.

"Don't worry about him; he's just warming up to everything. Give him time," I said with a smile that Rowen returned.

In the silence that followed, questions were asked and answered, and just when I thought Rowen would back out, Linden cleared his throat. "Pants off, Rowen. Sullivan wants you on his tongue. Unless you have any objection, I'd say he's earned it. He hasn't had the pleasure of seeing you come apart yet."

Rowen's lips parted, her pink tongue darting out in a quick swipe before, with a glance at the door, she released the button on her jeans and slid them down her hips.

"You barely survived the night. Are you sure you are up for this? What if I hurt you?"

Sullivan smirked and indicated to where the sheet was tenting in a way that assured everyone in the room that he was, indeed, up for anything. "Unless my heart stops beating, nothing would keep me from this. In fact, I'm counting on you making it difficult for me to breathe. Climb up."

Jeez. Somehow, she was hotter than ever in nothing but a t-shirt as she kneeled on the bed. "What about your shoulder?" she asked, brushing a hand over the bandages.

"I honestly could not care less. I'm on good pain meds, and all I need right now is you."

"I need you too," she murmured, looking down at him as though seeing him for the first time. Moving carefully, she crawled up the bed, looking to Linden for help as she straddled Sullivan's head. Linden moved in and guided her knee away from the shoulder injury, taking her elbow to help her balance as she faced the foot of the bed. Sullivan groaned, thrusting his hips beneath the blankets as he took an audible breath.

"Heaven," he murmured, turning his head to press a kiss to the inside of her thigh.

"Linden, could you move his blankets?" Rowen asked, grasping the headboard behind her and resisting Sullivan's attempts to pull her hips to his face.

"Just a minute," she said with a smile, pressing her palm to the center of his chest as Linden complied, going one step further and pulling Sullivan's hospital gown up to his waist, grasping his dick and pointing the head toward Rowen.

"Make him feel good."

I winced at the pain that lanced through my stomach as I rolled my hips at the sound of Linden's command. Unlike the others, I was in no condition for fun times, but Mr. Happy hadn't gotten the memo, and I was secure enough in my sexuality to admit Linden's controlling ways were a major turn-on. Reaching under my own gown, I squeezed the base of my cock to relieve the pressure as I watched Rowen's hair slide over her face, concealing the moment her mouth stretched around Sullivan's impressive length. Clearly, the guy was proportionate. Big guy, big dick. His attitude made a whole lot of sense now.

A small gasp left her as Sullivan pulled her down to his mouth and feasted. I remembered how she tasted. Sweet and salty and so freaking addictive that I envied Sullivan, but I was also so grateful that someone could be making our girl feel good in the moment. She deserved it.

They moved carefully together, and I gave up trying to control my reaction as the arousal created a pain all of its own. Stroking and squeezing, I fell into a rhythm that mirrored Rowen's undulations on the bed beside me. Her purring groans sent shocks of arousal through my body until a box of tissues appeared by my head.

"Thanks, man," I groaned, pulling a handful out and covering my head as the most painful orgasm ever rocketed through me.

For the record, masturbating less than twenty-four hours after getting stabbed is a really stupid idea.

In the aftermath, I waited for my vision to come back online as I tried to breathe through the pain.

"How you doin' there, pup?" Linden asked as Rowen screamed in pleasure and Sullivan moaned. Long streams of cum slashing over his stomach.

"Remind me not to get injured again. It fucking hurts."

Linden chuckled, taking the tissue box over to help Sullivan clean up his own mess.

"Thank you, doctor," Rowen said, grinning in a way that made my dick perk up again.

No. Too soon, man.

Linden grunted, watching her closely as she stepped off the bed. My breathing grew shallow as I watched her step right into Linden's space until she was pressed against his front. Dang. She looked hungry in that moment, and I recognized just how much she needed all of us. This was so right.

"I'm feeling a little empty, though. I've been licked and licked, but I haven't been filled since Zeph took me. What would you prescribe?"

Linden smirked.

"Miss Black, are you asking me to fuck you?"

"I'm asking you to fix what ails me, doctor. Are you qualified?"

Sullivan barked a laugh. "I think she wants to play doctor with you, Linden."

In a blink, Linden spun Rowen toward the bed, bending her over Sullivan's body so that her ass stuck out toward me. Man, Jett was missing out. I hoped he was all right out in the hall. Despite his protests, I knew damn well this was right up his alley. I couldn't wait to be healed enough to do some group stuff—if Rowen was up for it.

Linden stretched his body over Rowen, grinding his crotch against her ass.

"You're lucky I'm prepared this time, Miss Black. I think an internal exam might be just what you need."

Rowen groaned as Linden pulled back, sliding his wallet out of his pocket with one hand while thrusting two fingers into her pussy with the other.

"So tight," he praised as he withdrew a foil square and ripped it open with his teeth.

"Do you want my cock, Rowen?"

She mewled, pushing her hips back against his palm. I grinned in anticipation. Sure enough, his hand left her, only to crack across her ass. A rosy handprint appeared almost immediately, shining with her juices.

Sullivan scowled and moved to sit up. "Wait a minute."

"She knows the rules. Don't you, princess?" Linden massaged the red skin for a moment before pushing his fingers back inside her.

"Yes," she breathed, squirming.

"Good girl." He pumped into her a few more times before unbuttoning his slacks and sliding the condom down his length.

"Now. Tell me what you want, and I'll give it to you."

Rowen reached for his hips, but he moved them away and brought his hand down on her ass again. She moaned loudly, grasping Sullivan's sheets with desperate hands.

"I want you to fuck me in front of Sullivan and Zephyr. Please, Linden. I need you."

"Good girl," Linden repeated, moving in behind her and burying himself to the hilt in one stroke. Both of them cried out, and Sullivan groaned, his voice thick with arousal.

"Fuck, you're gorgeous," he muttered, stroking her face as Linden gave her a moment to adjust.

She leaned in to him and kissed him gently, including him in the moment of her joining with Linden. Pulling back, Sullivan locked eyes with Linden.

"Fuck her like I want to right now."

Linden nodded, guiding Rowen's hands to the railing on the bed, where she could get a strong grip.

"Don't let go."

He waited for her nod before pulling almost all the way out. On the next thrust, every thread of self-control seemed to evaporate as Linden gave himself completely to the moment.

It was wild. It was erotic, and even though only two people were a part of the action, the joining had an effect that made me feel a part of it too. I could only guess that Sullivan felt the same way as we watched our girl come apart under Linden's ministrations.

"I don't know if my legs will hold me," Rowen muttered, slumped over Sullivan's legs. I didn't really want her to stand—I had a great view of her ass—but she would probably need food soon.

"Did you want some of the breakfast you guys brought?" I asked.

"Good idea, pup," Linden said, helping Rowen upright and sliding her panties and jeans back on before fixing himself up. He pressed a kiss to her lips before moving across the room to the abandoned plastic bags she and Jett had brought in.

"I think the coffee may be cold, but—"

Jett burst into the room, cell phone in hand and a panicked look on his face.

"Just got a call from Makenna. We need to move now."

CHAPTER NINETEEN

Rowen

My happy, floaty feeling evaporated with Jett's appearance. Couldn't we catch a break?

I finally felt like we had all connected. Found the same page about our budding relationship, and now some other threat had come up. I shouldn't have been upset—I knew we had to find the source of the threat to truly be safe—but couldn't I have just a little breathing space after my guys killed Blade?

Linden pressed the cold cup of coffee into my hand, and I smiled gratefully. Coffee was coffee, and even cold, Australian coffee had American stuff beat. I took a big sip of the cold caffeine and tuned into Jett as he explained the call he had just received.

"... hospital records tampered with. She can't find the source, but she's working on it. For now, she's organized a camper van to be waiting for us outside in ten minutes. We need to get whatever medications you guys need and evacuate ASAP. Linden, can you organize meds while I get these guys up and going?"

Linden nodded and beelined for the door as Jett moved to help Zephyr sit up. Sullivan, unsurprisingly, had already removed the needle from his arm and was pushing up from the bed, looking around as though surprised his clothes weren't present.

"Looks like I'm leaving with my arse hanging out," he muttered.

Damn, we would have to go back to the hotel for our bags. Was it safe? Maybe Blade had missed some sort of check in and now someone else would just take his place.

Exhaustion hit so suddenly, I almost stumbled.

Why was this happening? What had I done to deserve this?

I looked around the room and couldn't regret what had come out of it, though.

A family.

"Makenna's ordered pickup for our bags, too. We'll have to inspect them for bugs before we move out, but we can't return to anywhere we've been since landing here. The plan is to drive. No set destination. She said she'd contact us when she knows more."

Dang, but Mak was a good friend. I'd have been dead by now for sure without her.

"She also said you need to ditch all your bank cards. Credit, debit, anything you've got, you need to destroy before we leave the city."

"How are we going to pay for anything?" I asked. I didn't want to emasculate any of the guys, but I had funds to burn and a blatant disregard for wealth. The others weren't as lucky.

"I can support us. It's kinda exciting to be the breadwinner of the family," Zephyr said, sucking in a sharp breath as Jett helped him to his feet.

"We appreciate it, pup. It won't be for long, though. Makenna's funneling funds for us so they can't be tracked. Plus, we can make our own way," Jett said. I understood the pride behind the statement, but did we really have that luxury?

"These people are hacking everything. They know all four of you are with me now, so I doubt it's safe for any of us to be funding much right now."

Sullivan grunted, holding the door open for Jett and Zephyr. "We'll deal with that when we come to it. For now, let's just concentrate on getting out of here."

"Good point. You're still on these people's kill list," Jett said, nailing Sullivan with a look as he guided Zephyr into the corridor.

Conversation died off between us as we navigated the corridors of the ward and did our best to avoid the eyes of curious inpatients. When the nurses' station came into view, I jumped ahead to field an irate staff member who didn't take kindly to two of her patients checking out against medical advice so soon after surgery.

"I'm sorry. But be assured we have qualified professionals who can attend to their care if you're worried about their wellbeing, but staying longer is not in their best interest."

The woman eyed the telephone on her desk, as though considering calling the authorities, but thankfully, my guys were already boarding the elevator. Rather than continuing the conversation, I shrugged an apology to the woman and jogged through the closing doors.

"Rowen, can you help Sullivan with Zephyr? I have a feeling we're going to have to go through security to get out of here."

"Can't we just talk to them?"

Jett and Sullivan both shook their heads. "We can't guarantee the staff haven't been compromised. Even if they aren't compromised, the longer we can keep our discharge off the books, the better chance we have of a clean getaway. If that means a couple of heads get cracked, so be it," Sullivan said, not quite hiding his wince as he accepted most of Zephyr's weight to free up Jett's hands. In case we needed to fight our way out.

How had things become so out of hand? The elevator chimed, announcing our arrival at ground level, and Jett moved into the widening gap the doors created.

Rounding the corner, the exit came into sight, and with it, two security guards, shoulder to shoulder.

"How can we help you, gents?" Jett asked loudly, moving to the center of the open space and drawing the men's attention away from where the three of us huddled.

Now was not the time to notice how damn attractive my soldier was, but he glowed with confidence as he controlled the room. The cheeky smile on his face seemed so out of place with the grumpy man I'd known. He was in his element, and I wondered exactly what his job had been in the Army. If we got out of this in one piece, I was going to make a better effort to know everything about these men who had so selflessly committed themselves to me.

"Time to move," Sullivan muttered, breaking me out of my thoughts as Jett and the guards moved away from the entrance.

Keeping an eye on the conversation unfolding on the other side of the lobby, we edged toward the glass sliding doors that would see us free. A click preceded the retracting door just as one guard turned back.

"Hey," he called, crossing to intercept us. His radio buzzed, pulling him up short. A tense moment passed as he asked his contact to repeat, then he turned to his companion with a bewildered look on his face. "They're cleared to leave."

"Go," Sullivan whispered, pushing Zephyr and me out the door without a backward glance.

"What was that?" I asked as Jett caught up to our group.

"Good timing, I'd say." Linden leaned against the brick siding of the hospital's main building with a Cheshire grin on his face, and a radio in hand. "Come on, the van's this way."

"Did you...?" I asked in shock, moving away from Zephyr as Jett took his weight.

"I might have had a disagreement with security when I was raiding the pharmacy. Seemed prudent at the time to gain access to their communications system. They were told to stand down before you got to the lobby. Seems someone else was pulling their strings, but they couldn't openly defy the direct order."

"But... how? Your voice—"

"My friend had a South African accent," Linden cut in, perfectly mimicking the accent in question.

Closing the distance between us, I stretched on tiptoe to press a quick kiss to his lips. "You're a genius, doc."

He chuckled and slapped my ass as I stepped into the camper van behind Jett and Zephyr. Up front, Sullivan shook hands with a guy in a hoodie with a grizzled beard and long brown hair who introduced himself as Doomslayer. Apparently Doomslayer knew Mak through the gaming community and owed her a solid after she saved his life and helped him win some game. I didn't really follow everything he said, but it was good news for us that he didn't see the difference between a virtual life debt and a real one. He seemed to find the cloak and dagger stuff fun, and even gave us his contact number in case we needed help with the authorities.

"What a nice dude," Zephyr observed from his slumped position behind the driver's seat.

Jett grunted something that could have been agreement or scorn as he methodically swept the van and our luggage, which Doomslayer had apparently picked up on his way through. With a final nod and awkward fist bump on Sullivan's side, Doomslayer moseyed off, casually pulling his hood up as Sullivan slid into the driver's seat.

"Jett, can you hook me up with some pants? I don't want to worry about crushing my nuts. They're rolling free in this stupid gown."

Jett made a noise that sounded strangely empathetic and tossed a pair of jeans that Sullivan easily snatched out of the air and slid up his long legs.

"Much better," he muttered, dumping his discarded gown behind him and starting the engine.

"There's twenty thousand dollars in the glovebox. Full tank of gas, and a roadmap under the passenger seat," Jett said, pulling a t-shirt out of his bag and passing it through to Sullivan. "The van is clear of bugs and tracking devices as far as I can see."

"Doomslayer told me Mak made him do an electronic sweep before he brought it around. He's handy, but the dude seriously has a warped sense of reality," Sullivan confirmed, his head popping through the neck hole as he steered one-handed into Sydney traffic. "Right. Do we want to head north? Or south? We can camp out somewhere overnight, but I'd prefer to get out of the city by at least a few hours before we stop for any kind of supplies. We'll grab a couple of burner cells later so Mak can contact us, too. Rowen? What do you think?"

All four guys locked onto me as though I had any answers in this situation. "Umm... north?" I was guessing. I had never been to Australia before, let alone explored enough to know where to go.

"Sweet. Sun and surf. Should be fun," Zephyr said, grin firmly in place despite his concerning pallor.

"You're not up for anything much past a nap right now. Take these like a good puppy," Linden said, moving in beside him and offering pills and a bottle of water.

"North it is," Sullivan muttered, pulling into the stream of traffic that flowed toward the iconic bridge and, hopefully, freedom.

"Jett, get your arse up here. You're co-pilot."

***

Over a six-week period, we traveled the northern reaches of Australia. Our bodies healed, and we grew closer as a group. It felt odd not to document every moment of our travels for public consumption, but I wanted these experiences to be just about us. For our eyes only.

There was also the fact the guys had unanimously voted against trying to continue the vlog series for all of our safety. Instead I took pictures, just for us, as we ambled along the coast line.

Linden vetoed Zephyr surfing in Queensland, but we all enjoyed a day out on the Great Barrier Reef on a boat that took us around to some of the islands, while local conservationists described the plant and animal life. We drove to Cape York, the northernmost tip of Australia, and looked out across the Torres Straight, trying to catch a glimpse of Papua New Guinea. We couldn't see it, but Jett, in a rare show of enthusiasm, entertained us with a story of the time he and some of his troops had walked the Kokoda trail as a team building exercise. I quietly added the hike to my bucket list, even though Sullivan insisted it was too dangerous to visit without a plan.

In Darwin, we swam with crocodiles and drank cocktails on Mitchell Street before heading inland to explore hidden places in Katherine and driving farther south to see Uluru.

My birthday found us in Fremantle, Western Australia, sipping ciders as we lounged in a quiet corner of the balcony of a bar and restaurant called the Sail and Anchor.

"Happy birthday, babe," Zephyr said, handing me a fresh drink so I wouldn't have to leave the comfort of Sullivan's lap. Leaning in, he took my mouth in a deep kiss that lasted long enough to heat my blood before squeezing onto the lounge chair beside Sullivan with a cheeky grin.

Jett leaned against the balcony railing, subtly surveying the street below as Sullivan and Linden discussed where to stay the night. Five people sleeping in a camper van was neither as romantic nor as comfortable as one would imagine. We slept two at a time when traveling—except for poor Sullivan, who barely fit in the bed alone—and camped out more often than not. The idea of a bed was incredibly attractive, but many of the local hotels were older and only offered double or queen-sized beds. I wished there was a way for all of us to spend the night together for my birthday, but it seemed like a dream that would have to wait for another year.

Taking a small sip of my drink, I startled as my ass began to vibrate. Sullivan groaned and shifted under me.

"Sorry," I said with a smirk that transformed into a grimace as I retrieved my cell and spotted the caller ID.

"Hello, Mother. It's been a while," I said, trying to keep the bitterness from my voice. I'd been away from New York for months, and while it wasn't uncommon to go long stretches without contact from the people responsible for my birth, I had reached out more than once to let them know people were trying to kill me. This was the first time they had responded.

"Don't be so dramatic, Rowen. It doesn't look good on you. I was calling to tell you you're done traipsing around the world. We need you at our charity ball next Saturday. Make sure you're back in New York by then."

"Thanks, Mom. I'm having a wonderful birthday. Thank you for asking."

"Rowen—"

"I will have to decline your kind invitation. I'm currently being hunted by killers, as I've told your messaging service several times."

A delicate sigh came down the line. "You're being ridiculous. Be at the Met at nine P.M. I'll have a dress delivered to your apartment."

"I'm on the other side of the world, Mom. I'm not going."

I counted down the seconds to my mother's detonation, but when her response came, it was in a tone I'd never heard before.

"Where are you?"

"Australia," I answered warily.

"Where in Australia? What town?"

"Um... Fremantle? It's on the west coast."

I wasn't sure how my city-loving mother would feel about her daughter touring the outback, but if I'd learned anything since I started this adventure, it was that I could choose who deserved my time and energy, and I'd given enough of it to the woman who thought I should be her display doll as compensation for her birthing me twenty-six years ago.

"Quaint," she said as I took a breath and prepared myself for the speech I'd been practicing.

"I want you to know, I forgive you."

Silence greeted the statement, and I knew I'd shocked her. In her world, she could do no wrong, so there would never be a need for forgiveness.

"I know you have always done what is best for you, even when it wasn't what was best for me, but I'm starting to understand it wasn't intentional. Some people put themselves in roles they're not suited for. Motherhood was something you were terrible at because while you always saw me as an extension of yourself, I am nothing like you. I'm my own person and that's okay. I spent years breaking my own spirit to fit into a mold you set for me. I developed a belief that if I wasn't exactly what everyone wanted me to be, I would be nothing, and I would be alone. I almost ruined the best things that ever happened to me because I expected them to react the same way you both always have. You aren't suited to the role of mother any more than I'm suited to the role of your daughter, so while I'll be eternally grateful for you giving me life and financial security, I learned everything important from friends that you scorned and four men I'll never let you meet. Please don't call me again. Our obligation to each other is finished."

I ended the call with shaking hands and sank back into Sullivan's warmth.

"Well done, *a pheata*. How do you feel?"

"Free."

CHAPTER TWENTY

Rowen

SULLIVAN'S FINGERS TRACED PATTERNS OVER MY BARE legs as we watched the sunset and chatted about where we wanted to head next. Linden wanted to explore the Swan Valley, while Jett thought it was time to leave the country. I expected Sullivan to side with Jett—he'd been increasingly anxious as we slowed our travels down to enjoy the sights of Down Under—but his attention seemed riveted on where his fingertips were inching under the leg of my loose linen shorts.

Subtly, I opened my knees, giving him the access he clearly wanted, and shivered as his hand inched toward the crease of my groin. Zephyr shifted beside us. Angling himself for a better view, he gripped my knee and urged me to open further as Sullivan's fingertips brushed my core over my panties.

Family drama was forgotten as I relaxed into my men's grips and allowed Sullivan to explore. In the corner of the balcony, with our backs to the rest of the clientele, I wasn't too worried about being seen by anyone outside of our little group, but the thrill that the possibility of discovery offered warmed my blood in ways I wasn't used to.

Jett looked to Sullivan for support in his argument and froze as he noticed what was happening across from him. His eyes heated, zeroing in on where Sullivan's hand disappeared beneath my clothing as though he could see through fabric if he just tried hard enough. Sullivan chuckled, the sound vibrating through my body and further revving me up as he deliberately removed his hand from the leg of my shorts and slid back inside from the waist, dipping inside my panties. I gasped as his fingers slipped over my sensitive skin, thrilled that I could share this with all of my men.

Linden glanced over, having thoroughly lost Jett's attention, and smirked. "Hold up."

Sullivan froze, cocking his head in question. Linden had a natural ability for controlling the room in intimate moments, and the guys had come to trust him and his dominant ways.

"Row, go to the powder room and take those panties off. Give Sullivan some room to work," Linden said, inclining his head toward the doorway behind me.

My cheeks tingled as I jumped to obey. A little too quickly, if the chorus of masculine chuckles I left behind was any indication. Inside, I found the facilities and slipped into the first available stall, baring my lower half and replacing my shorts, while I kept my already damp panties balled in a fist.

As calmly as I could, I headed back around the bar and outside to where four hungry sets of eyes tracked my approach. Linden's hand shot out as I stepped into the middle of our group, and I dutifully released what was in my hand. Maintaining eye contact, he brought the panties to his nose, inhaling loudly before tucking them into his pocket.

"Good girl. Now straddle Sullivan's lap facing me so we can watch him play with you. You know how Jett likes to watch."

I grinned at Jett's grunt of annoyance, but noticed his eyes didn't stray from my body as I followed Linden's directions. Zephyr gripped my calf in one big hand as Sullivan cupped my breast, squeezing gently before sliding his fingers down over my belly, lingering over the scarred tissue where the bullet had ripped through me, and dipping beneath my shorts. His hand definitely had room to move now. He traced my slit with one finger, intentionally disturbing the legs of my shorts and giving Jett and Linden teasing glimpses of what he was doing to my pussy.

"Is she wet?" Linden asked casually, sitting back and crossing his legs in a way that would look casual if I hadn't spotted the huge erection he was trying to hide from the innocent people drinking behind us.

"Soaked," Sullivan growled. "She's dripping down my hand. There's a good chance we'll leave a wet spot on these shorts. You know... I think she likes being watched."

He leaned in toward my ear, his beard scratching along my hairline. "Or maybe she likes the danger of being caught. Are you an exhibitionist, Rowen?"

My breath caught on a moan as he slowly pushed two fingers inside me. Sullivan was big all over, and his fingers stretched me in a way that had me squirming as he set a lazy pace, stroking in and out, as though happy to stay there for a while.

"Why do all of you have so much patience?" I growled, shifting my hips in an attempt to take control.

"I don't," Zephyr said with a shrug.

I eyed him thoughtfully. He didn't have patience, but he seemed to enjoy taking cues from the others, which often led to him waiting happily. Who was I kidding? Zephyr was always happy.

"Is that you offering to put your head between my thighs and put me out of my misery?" I asked hopefully as Sullivan continued to move his fingers in slow, deep thrusts, his thumb brushing over my clit on every other stroke. Zephyr groaned and looked hopefully at Sullivan, who shook his head.

"She's not finishing yet, pup. You can have a taste if you want, though." He pulled his hand from my pants and offered it to Zephyr, who sucked Sullivan's wet fingers into his mouth without hesitation.

"Jesus, I won't need your hand to come if you two keep that up," I muttered, watching Zephyr's tongue flick out to collect the wetness on the side of Sullivan's wrist.

"I think it's time we find a hotel," Jett rumbled, his voice the deep bass that told me he was beyond turned on.

"Yes, please," I said, my voice so breathy I wasn't sure they heard me.

***

I couldn't have said what woke me in the early hours of the morning, but I had been dreaming of my guys, a wonderful reimagining of all the things they had done to me the night before, when I became aware that my bed was empty and there was a strangely familiar smell in the air. My brain scrambled, alarm bells ringing in my mind as I tried to orient myself in the unfamiliar hotel room. Zephyr and Linden had been sharing the bed with me after our earlier session, Sullivan and Jett having offered to share the room next door. They were two peas in a pod, the soldier and the bounty hunter. After a rocky start, the two had bonded over a mutual protective streak a mile long, and, oddly, a shared sense of humor.

My attention was forcibly returned to the dark room as I jarred my fingers on the wall. Hissing in pain, I smoothed my hand along the surface until I hit a bump in the wall, which, after further exploration, turned out to be a switch. With a sigh, I flicked the light on and immediately noticed a haze in the air.

Unease crawled up my spine as the lights dimmed and flickered.

Time to find the guys.

When I opened the door into the corridor, a heavy dark cloud rolled over me, forcing me back as I dropped to my knees, hacking and coughing. The smoke filled my room quickly, smothering me as I tried to draw enough air into my lungs. *Move*, I screamed at myself mentally. Smoke meant fire. Fire meant I had to get the hell out of there. The question was where? Had the guys gotten out?

Crawling slowly down the hall, keeping my head as close to the carpet as I could in an effort to find fresh air, I hugged the wall, searching for the next doorway down, where I couldn't decide if I wanted to find my men or not. If they were there, we were all in danger. If they weren't... where were they?

My first question was answered as I fell through the void of their doorway, head first into a room with a perfectly made up bed that was decidedly empty of human life.

My throat burned, my lungs aching, as I pulled my t-shirt over my nose to try to filter the air. I had to get out; that much was certain. I could find the guys once I could breathe again.

Head swimming in a way that made me want to lie down and rest a moment, I forced stinging eyes open and pulled myself back into the hall. Where was the exit?

Our rooms were on the third floor, and I knew turning left out of our doorway would lead to a bank of elevators, but had the emergency exit been that way? Or at the opposite end of the hall?

The temperature in the hall was steadily rising, and my arms and forehead dripped with sweat. I couldn't tell where the fire was and could only pray it wasn't between me and safety.

My head thumped with a lancing pain that increased by the moment so that I could barely keep my eyes open, but I continued my slow crawl toward the end of the hall. Oddly, Semme's "Do Dat (Stop, Drop and Roll)" started repeating in my head. *You're delirious, just get to the exit.*

With my waning strength, I pushed through the door at the end of the hall and spilled onto a concrete stairwell in a mess of arms and legs. The air quality in here wasn't much of an improvement, but at least I had a way down. Half stumbling, half sliding, I rushed to the ground floor, clutching the banister for support as my legs threatened to collapse beneath me. My descent ended in an alcove with a single heavy door. Pushing at the handle, I sank to my knees, my breath leaving me on a sob as the metal remained stubbornly closed beneath my hands.

Hot, aching, half blind, and unable to catch a breath, I slumped against the nearest wall and eyed the door. So close. I was so close to freedom.

I wondered if my parents would care if I didn't make it. Probably not. I'd made it clear I wasn't going to play by their rules anymore. They would probably find a way to use it to their advantage. Hold a fundraiser, or... I shut that thought down immediately. No sense using my final moments to contemplate people who didn't deserve the energy. Instead, I thought of a grumpy soldier. A talented doctor. A soft-hearted bounty hunter. An heir who hadn't been corrupted by life. Each of my men flashed before my eyes in a montage that would have made me cry if my tears hadn't been burned away.

I could almost hear Zephyr's voice as I closed my eyes to see them better. The heat rose further, and I realized Zephyr's voice wasn't my imagination. Why was he yelling? Right. The burning building. With a herculean effort, I raised my fist and hammered on the door beside me. My throat was raw, my voice long gone. But maybe...

Everything outside went quiet, and after a moment, I let my hand drop. They hadn't heard me. After all we'd been through, I was going to be the one to leave. My chest rattled with a cough as I dropped my shirt away from my mouth.

"Rowen." The voice sounded panicked.

My body was jostled, and suddenly cool air danced along my skin. I became weightless as strong arms lifted me, taking me away from the heat and suffocating smoke and laying me on soft, cool grass.

"I've got her."

CHAPTER TWENTY ONE

Linden

"Give her some room," I growled, pushing past Zephyr to check Rowen's pulse.

"She looks cold," the kid offered.

"She's cyanosed," I muttered, counting out her heartbeats and wishing I had a clock to better check her progress. "Too much smoke in her lungs means too little oxygen in her bloodstream. Where the hell are the paramedics? And why didn't an alarm go off? The entire building is on fire."

Rowen's heartbeat was slow but steady. Her breathing rough but improving the longer we sat in the fresh air, downwind of the fire that had reached the roof, sending ashes spiraling on the early morning breeze out over the water toward Rottnest Island.

"She'll be okay," I decided, sitting back on my heels. Zephyr nodded and glanced at my other patient.

Sullivan had a deep purple bruise forming over his left ear, a result of blunt force trauma we were too slow to prevent.

"Who do you think they were?"

"The same people we've been running from for months. The question is, how did they find us?"

With a violent surge, Sullivan shot upright beneath my hands, fists up and snarling.

"Easy, big guy," I said as he focused on me, then Zephyr, then Rowen, who was still unconscious, though breathing better every minute.

"What...?"

"Happened?" I finished for him.

He nodded.

Where to start? I barely understood the events of the last half hour, and I wasn't sporting a concussion.

***

After wearing Rowen out in bed, Jett and Sullivan had gone back to their room, and Zephyr and I had stayed with our girl, playing cards as she slept. Around midnight we'd headed to bed, and I'd woken to the sound of footsteps outside our room. Recognizing the voices engaged in a hushed conversation, I stepped out into the hall.

"We're going out for a smoke," Jett said as soon as he spotted me.

"Why? Neither of you smoke."

Jett rubbed his neck and glanced toward the elevators. "I quit a while ago. I only really do it when I'm anxious. Used to light up a ton on deployment, but something is bugging me tonight. Can't you feel it?"

I shook my head. Rowen was happy, and we were all finding our feet with this new relationship. From my perspective, life was good. I'd feel better if we'd had a progress report from Makenna, but no news was good news, right?

"It's like the silence before the mortar strike. The animals know, see. They all clear out and you're left with this eerie peace where there should be the chaos of nature. I feel like we're waiting for the first explosion, but I can't see the threat. Shit, maybe it's PTSD finally catching up with me, but I need to unwind if I want any chance of sleep."

Sullivan clapped him on the shoulder, and the two continued on as I headed back into the room. Jett's words circled through my mind, infecting me with his paranoia until a glance at the bed confirmed I wouldn't be able to lie down and find sleep again.

Maybe I should have gone with the guys.

Wandering to the window, I watched them emerge from the hotel below, saw the flare of a lighter, and watched them walk to the edge of the pool of light cast by the hotel's entrance, cherry red lights swinging at their sides. It still felt surreal, seeing these two sides of my life get along so well. The military had taught me a moral code that was missing from my formative years in the foster system, but it had also taught me to be tough and do what was needed. Offering back room care to those who were on the wrong side of the law was something that I had always justified with the stance that if I could help, I would. Sullivan had always been different to some of the other unsavories I'd treated, though I'd never tell him so, but that didn't mean I could ever have predicted the friendship that had sprouted between him and the strait-laced—

My thoughts cut off as I caught movement in the shadows of the trees that separated the carpark from the hotel grounds. Late night arrivals? Early morning joggers, maybe? Damn Jett, he really had got in my head. Trying to relax, I watched Sullivan tip his head back and send a cloud of smoke skyward, but I found that my attention strayed back to the trees time and again.

Behind me, the bed creaked. Zephyr pulled himself upright and shuffled toward the ensuite, unaware of my attention on him. He was a good kid. Our doubts about him had been unfounded as we realized his positivity was a choice and not a sign of stupidity. He had a way of focusing on the good and enjoying even the most mundane activities as long as he was surrounded by the people he cared about, and apparently, that was all of us, not just Rowen. Pretty wise for a twenty-one year old, if you asked me. I wasn't that smart at his age.

As the flush of a toilet sounded behind the closed door, I glanced out the window and panicked. A dark shadow the size of a large man lay beyond the light of the entrance, and across the grass, heading for the treeline were shadows moving in a lumbering way, as though dragging something.

"Hey, what's—?"

Bolting past Zephyr on the way for the door, I ignored his enquiry. No time. I hit the emergency stairwell, taking the steps two at a time and flying the exit door at a run. The second slam of the door a moment later told me Zephyr was behind me as backup.

I reached the spot I had last seen the guys and looked past the flickering edge of light, out toward the darkness in hopes of finding the shadows I had spotted before.

"Why does it smell like gasoline?" Zephyr asked, jogging up. "There!" he yelled, pointing toward a dark shape lumbering through the trees.

Instead of trying for any kind of stealth, we charged across the lawn and threw ourselves at the two men dragging what turned out to be Sullivan's limp form. At the sight of our approach, both men dropped the dead weight and tore off toward an idling van with back doors open wide. Skidding on my knees, I slid in next to Sullivan and checked for a pulse as Zephyr flew past me, angling for the men who were already leaping into the vehicle as it rolled toward the parking lot entrance, gathering speed as they slammed the doors.

Sullivan's pulse was strong, his breathing steady. As I checked his body for trauma, I found a laceration to the base of the skull with swelling present, small scrapes on his arms and legs from being dragged across the lawn, and a cell phone in his pocket. Using the flashlight app, I confirmed his pupils were slightly uneven in size but responsive to light. Concussed, but hopefully not too badly. I would be able to tell more once he regained consciousness.

Zephyr returned, breathing hard and holding his side. "I think they got Jett," he said, casting worried eyes at Sullivan. My frustrated curse was drowned out by a roar of sound from behind me. Zephyr's face dropped, and I knew, even before I turned around, that our night was only getting worse. The entrance of the hotel was ablaze. Red and orange flames licked the chandelier by the reception desk, and from our vantage point, we could see window dressings curling in the heat on the second floor.

"Rowen," we said in unison, both sprinting for the building, unsure how we could get to her. We had to get her out safely. There was no other option.

"What do we do?" Zephyr asked, looking up at the third story window that we knew our girl was sleeping behind. It didn't look like the fire had reached that high yet, but it was only a matter of time.

"We have to find a way in."

Heading in opposite directions, we skirted the building, searching for an alternate entrance. All the while pleading to whatever deity might listen that both Rowen and Jett came out of this all right. Shit. This was all so fucked up.

When I'd made it three quarters of the way around the building, I found Zephyr prying at the exit door we had used earlier.

"Help me," he called, beating at the door with a rock.

"That won't work. We need something to pry it open." Sticks littered the ground nearby, and I looked around, hoping for a better option. Shit, we were wasting time.

Zephyr pointed out a park bench that we could try to pull apart.

Screw it.

Crossing to the bench, we pulled at it with bare hands, trying to leverage the wooden panels away from the steel. After a couple of minutes with little progress, Zephyr picked something out of the grass and used it as leverage.

"What's that?" I asked.

"Piece of metal I just found on the ground."

I stared at him for a moment before snatching the tool from his hands and rushing back to the door.

"I swear, pup. You're the dumbest smart person I've ever met," I grunted, slipping the metal into a dent in the door and working it open.

"You think I'm smart?" Zephyr asked, grin fading as the door popped open to reveal an unconscious Rowen on the other side.

"Bring her down to where we have Sullivan. I'll check her out there. Is there any chance you got the plates of that van? We need to see if Makenna can work her magic."

Four of us were safe, but four out of five wasn't good enough. Jett was missing, and we needed to know who was responsible.

***

Palming Sullivan's cell, I checked Rowen's breathing again and moved away a little to place the call. Before I could do anything, the device buzzed in my hand. Makenna's name flashed across the screen and I wondered for a moment if she was psychic, or if more shit had gone wrong that we didn't yet know about.

"Hey, it's Linden," I answered.

"Get out of the hotel now! Your position is compromised. Ditch this cell and drive in any direction. It doesn't matter where, but you need to move."

"You're too late." Hanging my head, I realized my feet were bare. My toes were crusted with soil from running all over the property.

"They got Jett. Burned the hotel. Fuck, Mak, tell me you know who's doing this."

"Rowen...?"

"Is safe. She's inhaled some smoke but is otherwise fine. She's recovering on the lawn. What is going on here? Have you found anything?"

A heavy sigh came down the line, followed by the clicking of a keyboard.

"I don't have anything concrete, but my working theory isn't pretty, and I'm worried about how Rowen will react."

I glanced over my shoulder and eased a little farther away from the group. "What do you mean?"

"I've been diving into their servers, picking up some of their communications with the details Sullivan gave me. That's how I found out about the orders for tonight, but these guys are good. I mean really good. There are some lines of encryption even I haven't been able to crack. Whoever is behind this is unbelievably smart. I'd love to get into their heads and figure out their methods for—"

"Makenna."

"Sorry. Anyway, they had this folder with press releases. One of them was an announcement for a charity called Never Alone. They support parents who've lost their children. But this whole press release is about how Rowen is attending with her parents and what a great relationship they all have. It has quotes from them saying things like how they can't imagine having to live without their daughter.

"Look, I could be completely paranoid here, but I know what that family is like. Rowen and I have been besties for years, and those people don't give a shit about her. What they do care about? Control and appearances. Linden, what if...?" The unfinished sentence hung in the air, the unspoken accusation loud as the inferno that consumed the building behind us.

"Her mom called for her birthday yesterday," I whispered, remembering Rowen's bid for independence, and her happiness at thinking herself finally free.

Surely, her parents couldn't be that cold. No one could meet Rowen and not fall immediately in love with her spirit. The fact I was sharing her with three other men should have been commentary enough on her allure.

"When was Never Alone registered as an entity? Who is on the papers?" I asked, grasping at straws. There had to be another explanation.

A few clicks later, Makenna cursed and murmured something that sounded like, *"Where are my kisses?"*

"Makenna?"

"Gimme a minute. I can't deal with this without chocolate. The organization was founded three months ago. It's listed under a shell company. I can run the financials and follow the money back to the owners, but I think we know where it'll lead."

A ping came down the line, and Makenna gasped so hard she choked. Coughing hard, she wheezed in a breath, even as her keyboard started clicking again.

"Neve and Rayleigh O'Shea. Do those names ring any bells?"

Farther up the lawn, Sullivan was hunched over Rowen, whose head was moving as though she were starting to come around.

"They're supposed to be ghosts to the rest of the world."

"Well, these ghosts are on the bad guys' radar. If we want to keep them breathing, I think we need to move them."

"Make it happen. I'll make sure Sullivan contacts them so they can be prepared. Who's paying for all this, anyway?"

Makenna snorted. "People who can afford it, trust me. Speaking of money, I've created a new account for Rowen that is ready as soon as she wants it. I know a guy who can make some new IDs for you, too. For now, tell me what you know about the guys who took Jett."

CHAPTER TWENTY TWO

Rowen

"WE CAN'T LEAVE," I ARGUED AGAIN, MY SMOKE-roughened voice nearly inaudible over Sullivan's fretting. I understood his concern; his family had been threatened at home, Jett was gone, and there was a better than good chance my parents were responsible for the hit that had been put out on me. Complicated didn't even begin to describe the situation.

Hunkered in our camper van at a beach in Rockingham, thirty minutes south of Fremantle, we tried to decide on our next move. Mak hadn't been able to find the van that took Jett, but I refused to believe they'd gone far. I was the one they wanted.

"We can't stay," Linden countered. "They're going to come back for you, and next time, we might not be so lucky."

"I'm not leaving Jett with them." My voice broke, the strain of emotion and the raw state the smoke had left my throat in too much to carry the words. Pushing to my feet, I stomped out of the van and headed toward the sand.

"Let her go," Zephyr murmured.

I pulled my shoes off, tossing them back toward the vehicle, and moved down the shore until seafoam washed over my toes. The sunrise was still little more than a tease, a slight change in the deep blues and purples of the night sky. My skin rippled with goosebumps as the first seagulls screamed good morning in the cool predawn air. There had to be a way to find Jett.

As I wriggled my toes in the sand, wondering where they could have taken my soldier, the sun made its grand appearance in a splash of golden glory that reached up through the layers of night, spreading colors across the sky that were eerily similar to the flames of the night before.

Caught as I was in the glory of the new day, I didn't notice the vibration in my pocket at first. When I realized my cell was ringing, my first thought was of my parents asking me home. Truth be told, they had never been my home. Sullivan, Linden, Zephyr... Jett. These men were my home. The same way Makenna and Sloane had always been my family. Screw genetics.

I pulled the cell phone out of my pocket, another iteration of the speech I had given my mother the night before poised on the tip of my tongue.

"Rowen Black." The voice was decidedly not my mother's. The deep baritone belonged to a male I was sure I'd never met.

"Where's Jett?" I demanded. No one else should have had this number. No one else would be calling at five A.M. for a chat.

"So you did survive the fire. No matter."

"Where's Jett?" I asked again. Anxiety stole my patience as it occurred to me that someone who could set fire to an entire building, who clearly didn't care about casualties, had one of the men I loved.

Loved.

Shit, I did love him, and I hadn't had the chance to tell him. Jett, of all of my guys, needed to know he was loved. I knew he was still hurt over what happened with Kylie and Felix, more because he lost the friendship with his brother than anything else, and he'd jumped feet first into a relationship where he was sharing me with three other guys.

They had walked away from their lives, all intent on protecting me. Hell, Sullivan's mother and sister were now under threat because he had gone rogue for me.

It was my turn to look after them.

"Let him go and you can have me instead."

"We don't want him. Be at the B shed ferry terminal at ten A.M. If you're late, we'll shoot him. If you aren't alone, we'll shoot him. If you try to call the police—"

"You'll shoot him. I got it. I'll be there, but I want proof of life now. Let me talk to him."

Silence.

The call had been terminated.

The tremors started in my stomach, some fault line in the very core of me threatening to rupture. Six weeks I had been given to experience life with these wonderful men. Six weeks of love and acceptance, of adventure and discovery. Six weeks of feeling like my life was whole, and in one night, everything had changed.

Drawing the salty air as deeply into my lungs as I could and forcing the rising panic attack into submission, I focused on the cool sand beneath my toes.

I would say goodbye to the others first.

Hands slid around my waist, and I turned into the embrace, kissing the down-turned corner of Zephyr's mouth.

"I don't like seeing you scowl," I whispered, wrapping my arms around his neck and pulling him into my kiss.

Desperation marked every thrust of my tongue, and as a whimper left me, he hoisted my legs around his hips and carried me back up the beach. Pressing my back into the side of the van, he held me in place with his hips as he took control of the kiss. Between my thighs, his erection pressed tight against my clit, dragging a gasp from me as I rocked into him in search of friction. I needed more. Everything he had to give, and maybe more than that.

"Zephyr," I moaned, letting my head drop back against the van as his mouth traveled down my neck and over my collarbone.

"I know, babe," he muttered in between kisses and lifted a fist to bang against the paneling.

"What, pup? Oh..." Sullivan trailed off as our eyes connected. In the space of a heartbeat, I silently begged him to join us, holding out a hand to him as I continued to shamelessly ride Zephyr through our clothing.

"Bring her inside. We'll make it work."

I realized what he meant a moment later when we stepped into the van to find Sullivan stretched out on the available floor space and Linden rifling through one of the overhead cupboards. A moment later, he turned with condoms and lube in hand.

"No condoms, please. I... I just need to be close to you all right now. Is that okay?"

I didn't know how they would react. With our unexpectedly long stay in Australia, they knew I had no birth control. I couldn't exactly tell them that it didn't matter because I'd probably be dead before a fetus could be conceived, but I wasn't lying about needing to be close. I wanted them in me as deep as they could go.

"It's your body. I'm clean, for what it's worth, and we can get a morning-after pill if we need to," Linden said slowly, glancing at the others before returning the condoms to the cupboard.

"I'm clean too. I got tested just before I was assigned to... you," Sullivan piped up from the floor, brow creasing as he considered the implications of his assignment.

I ran a hand down Zephyr's jaw, then dropped to the floor to kiss Sullivan's frowning mouth. "I trust you. I want to be with all of you. At the same time. Linden, can we do that?" I hoped he understood what I meant.

Over the previous weeks we had experimented together, had had sex and performed oral until I'd been boneless with satisfaction, and Linden had been the controlling force in all our group activities. He'd insisted on easing me into the kinkier side of things, but if this was the last time I saw them, I didn't want to hold back.

"We can do whatever you want, as long as you're comfortable. Are you okay? It's been a big morning," he said, crouching to my level.

I couldn't maintain eye contact while I lied; so instead, I focused on my hands, pushing Sullivan's t-shirt up, and pasted on a smile. "I'm fine. I just want to feel close to you guys right now."

Sullivan lifted his head and shoulders to help with the clothing removal, then returned the favor, trailing kisses along my skin as he revealed it to the eyes in the van.

"Geez, you're beautiful," Zephyr muttered as my hair slipped free of my shirt.

I flashed a more genuine smile over my shoulder and wriggled backward until I was sitting on Sullivan's legs and could work his pants down. Swiping my hair to one side, I bent over his growing erection, running my tongue up his length in long, lazy strokes. His skin felt soft under my tongue—such a contrast to the hard muscle beneath. In the van's interior, his panting breaths were loud as the others sat back, content to watch while I played.

"You're enjoying the torture, aren't you?" Linden drawled after a while, his expression intense as Sullivan lifted his hips, the head of his cock dipping into my mouth and leaving a trail of salty precum on my chin.

"Suck him all the way in and lift your ass up so Zephyr can take off your shorts."

It was a little awkward to keep Sullivan in my throat while maneuvering out of my bottoms, but once I was free, Zephyr wasted no time burying his face in my pussy. I groaned around Sullivan's girth, pulling off for a moment to drop down and suck his balls into my mouth one at a time while stroking the skin behind his sack with two fingers. The movement conveniently pushed me more firmly against Zephyr's tongue.

"Here, pup," Linden said.

In the next moment, the warmth of Zephyr's mouth was gone, replaced with the cool sensation of lube drizzling down my ass crack.

"Rowen, do you want Zephyr to stretch your ass?" Linden asked in a level tone.

I moaned, causing Sullivan to break into a full-body shudder. A loud crack flew through the air, and I pulled back sharply as Sullivan shouted in outrage. "No spanking while my balls are in her mouth, kid! What if she bit down?!"

Zephyr grinned, unrepentant. "She didn't use her words."

Linden chuckled as I narrowed my eyes at the sunny boy, who was showing a darker side. "Anyone would think you like punishing me."

His grin grew even wider. "Oh, I do. Don't let the nickname fool you; this puppy bites."

To prove his point, he leaned forward and took the flesh of my ass between his teeth in a hard nip before soothing it with his tongue. I groaned, leaning into the sensation, especially when one finger came up to circle my back entrance.

"Please," I whispered, pushing my hips back as he continued to brush over my sensitive flesh.

"What do you want, Rowen?" Linden asked, looking casual as you please, while leaning against the bunk and watching the others play.

I huffed. "Zephyr, will you please stretch my ass so that you and Sullivan can fuck me at the same time, then Linden can replace whoever comes first? I need you guys in me, like, yesterday."

"We can't do yesterday, but as for the rest..." Zephyr trailed off as he eased his finger inside me.

The sensation was foreign, but not unpleasant. He pumped a couple of times before pulling out to add more lube. I relaxed into the feeling and returned to torturing Sullivan with my tongue. Before long, it didn't feel like enough.

"More," I grunted, pushing back against Zephyr's hand.

"Fuck, I'm tapping out. I'll come before I get inside you if you keep going," Sullivan said, pulling Linden forward by the pant leg. "Give her something to suck on while pup adds another finger."

Steadying myself on Linden's belt, I pulled him closer, opening his zipper and fishing out what I wanted.

Zephyr added more lube and continued to stretch me, scissoring his fingers in a way that drove me to the brink of madness.

"I'm ready. Fuck, I'm ready. Take me, please." I kissed the tip of Linden's cock and settled back, presenting my ass to Zephyr.

"I think you might need Sullivan in first if you want us both, babe," he offered, continuing to move his fingers inside me in a lazy rhythm.

If that's what we needed to get the show on the road...

In a fluid move, borne of practice from the last few weeks, I brought Sullivan's tip to my core and eased down his length. Dual sighs filled the air as I began to move on him, reacquainting myself with his size. Linden stroked himself with an unhurried pace as we got ready, and then Zephyr was behind me, tight against my back. At his urging, I leaned over Sullivan's chest, hissing with pleasure as he pushed inside. I felt full, whole in a way I never had before, and as they started moving in a counter rhythm, I felt close to tears. This was the only time I would ever have this.

"Are you okay?" Linden asked, watching me too closely for comfort.

I nodded, pulling him close so I could take him back into my mouth. Pushing my hair from my eyes, he tried to look into me, through me, but there was only one thing I wanted him to see.

Love. Pure and simple.

With a soft smile, he cupped my jaw, stroking the seal my lips formed around his cock with a look in his eyes that bordered on worship.

"I love you too," he whispered a moment before Zephyr shouted, his fingers tightening on my hips as he pumped out his release. Pulling out gently, he pressed a kiss to the center of my spine before backing off to give us more room.

"Linden," I started when he made no move to replace him.

"You might be sore," he hedged, frowning in concern.

"I'm not. Actually, there's something I'd like to try." Sullivan's thrusts slowed to a stop as I eyed the men in front of me. "I want you both in me at the same time."

"Didn't we just..."

"No," I interrupted Sullivan's confused protest. "I want both of you in my pussy. Is that clear enough?"

Linden and Sullivan exchanged glances. "I already feel as mentally stretched as I can manage. I want you to physically stretch me. Please."

Linden watched me for another minute before nodding. "We'll give you anything you want, but we need to use lube. That's a nonnegotiable. I don't want to hurt you."

I nodded. That was fine. I moved off Sullivan while they got ready and almost swallowed my tongue when Linden casually reached out and lubed Sullivan's dick for him.

"That was hot," Zephyr mumbled from the front corner of the van in a way that made me think he was taking notes. The mental image of Zephyr drawing diagrams like our intimate times were some kind of sex school made me snort, causing my lubed-up-and-ready men to throw matching, confused looks my way.

Linden shook it off first, moving behind me and guiding me back into position over Sullivan. "Take him first again. I'll move in after."

I nodded and once again sat on Sullivan's dick, leaning forward to give Linden room. The stretch was different this time. If I were honest, my ass was a little lonely after all the attention it had gotten earlier, but once Linden was fully seated, I had to take a moment to breathe. Neither of these guys was small.

"So tight," Sullivan grunted, shifting beneath me. "You might have to ride us, Row."

I sat up carefully, looping my arms around Linden's neck as he cupped my breasts, and moved over their cocks in an undulating rhythm that took me to the edge and over it before I knew what was happening.

My orgasm broke me.

Screaming in pleasure and the pain I couldn't keep hidden any longer, tears streamed down my face as I sobbed through the most intense experience of my life. Linden and Sullivan followed almost at once, shaking and growling through their own releases. In the aftermath, I couldn't rein in the tears.

"Did we break her?" Zephyr whispered, stroking my back in anxious circles.

"No, she just had an intense experience. It's not uncommon to have this kind of reaction. Can you make her a hot chocolate? The sugar will do her good. We'll get her cleaned up and warm." Linden scooped me up and rearranged me in Sullivan's lap as he prepared a warm washcloth and cleaned me up with gentle strokes.

"I don't know why I'm still crying," I lied, snuggling into Sullivan's warmth as Linden finished cleaning my pussy and rinsed the cloth before returning to clean the cum from my ass. I wondered if I should have been embarrassed by any of it, but took my cue from the guys, who all seemed relaxed.

How could I leave them?

The answer was: I had to. As amazing as this experience had been, there was still a piece of my heart missing, and I intended to get it back.

Even if it meant I wouldn't be around to experience the wholeness.

CHAPTER TWENTY THREE

Rowen

My chance to slip away came an hour later. As I was anxiously watching the clock and imagining the time until Jett's demise slowly melting into the void, Linden and Sullivan decided to go on a breakfast run.

"Bacon?" Sullivan asked me with a cheeky quirk to his brow.

"Always," I said, pulling him down for a kiss.

"I love you," I whispered against his lips, thrusting my tongue into his mouth to avoid hearing him return the words. I needed them to know how I felt, but it seemed unfair to have them confess something so big when I was about to do something so life-changingly stupid.

Once they were out of sight, I slipped into Zephyr's lap where he sat near the front of the van reading a real life newspaper.

"You know you can get that on the internet, right?" I teased.

"Yeah, but you can recycle this one. My dad used to read the newspaper every morning over breakfast when I was a kid. I guess it reminds me of him. Just don't tell the others I flipped straight to the comic strips."

I glanced over my shoulder to see he was, in fact, reading *Calvin and Hobbs*. A laugh burst out of me before I could stop it. Zephyr had a remarkable ability to make me feel light as a feather, even in the heaviest of situations.

"I love you," I blurted.

The grin that stretched across his face was both the lights of home and a transcendent experience I'd never tire of.

"I—"

I cut him off with a kiss. If anyone could convince me there was another way to get Jett back, it was Zephyr. But it could cost Jett's life, and that outcome was unacceptable.

"I'm going to go for a quick walk down the beach before the guys get back," I said as calmly as I could, sliding off his knee and heading for the door.

"I'll come with you."

"No. You stay and read your comic. Let me know what the tiger gets up to later, okay?" The smile I gave him felt brittle as glass, but I managed to escape without further comment.

Earlier, I had googled the ferry terminal I was supposed to meet them at and worked out where the train station was in Rockingham. My original plan was to hop a train to Fremantle, but once I was seated in a taxi I'd flagged down, I decided to simplify the plan and asked the driver to take me directly to the meeting place. Nine thirty flickered on the old digital clock on the dash, and I picked at my nails, anxiety rising. What if it was all for nothing? He could be dead already, or I could be late and see him die.

"Can you go any faster?" I asked the driver, ignoring his scowl in favor of bouncing my knee and staring out the windscreen as though I could will the terminal closer.

At nine fifty-nine, we pulled up at a building that was little more than an oversized shed. I threw a handful of money in the driver's direction and all but threw myself out of the cab, running before the door was closed for the nearest entrance. The few people I had seen on the street disappeared altogether as I stepped through the open doors into a deserted space.

"Hello?" I called, shivering despite the warmth of the day outside. Wandering through the building and out toward the water, I jumped and almost screamed as someone tall and very unfamiliar stepped in behind me.

"Get in the boat. We're going for a ride."

"Where's Jett?" I asked, half turning before a rough hand pushed me forward. At the base of a rusted ladder, whose bottom rungs kissed the waterline, was a small motorboat that barely looked seaworthy.

"You want to see your boyfriend, you'll get in and give me no more grief."

This was a bad idea, but out of options, I complied. Halfway down the ladder, my ass started to buzz, and not in the well-used-this-morning kind of way. In my distraction, I hadn't noticed I'd pocketed my cell instead of leaving it as I'd planned. Shit, the guys were going to be mad. It buzzed five times before falling still, and I breathed a sigh of relief as my escort hit the bottom of the ladder and jumped into the boat, sending the vessel rocking in an alarming manner.

Once we were situated, he turned the boat's nose for the horizon and took off.

Too soon, the land fell away over the horizon, and I shivered at the sheer amount of water around us. I loved to swim, but not knowing how much water was beneath you, and what inhabited it, was a disconcerting thing. My cell started up again, buzzing five times before falling silent, and I watched my companion closely to see if he had noticed. Nothing. Looked like the boat's noisy old motor was good for something at least.

After what felt like a lifetime to my overstressed mind, a catamaran appeared on the horizon. Its huge dual hulls loomed over us as we passed across the bow and pulled up to stairs at the back of the craft.

"Climb up," my companion grunted, poking me in the back when I didn't move fast enough.

Given the choice between the luxury yacht full of danger and a boat in danger of sinking into untold depths, I opted to climb onto the relatively stable deck above me. As I ascended the final step, a vicious curse sent my heart soaring even as my stomach dropped to my feet.

"Jett," I whispered, wanting to run to him, even as I was grabbed and all but thrown across the deck.

In the hours since I'd seen Jett, he clearly hadn't waited quietly. Blood streaked his hair, and his face was more purple than white, a mottled mess of fresh bruising that made me want to cry. The flow of curse words that left his mouth would have made my mother faint if she were in the company of her peers. Despite being tightly bound to one of the deck fixtures, he threw himself around with a violence that made me worry he'd hurt himself.

Hurt himself more. I amended, as he twisted enough to show the raw mess his wrists had become.

"You said he can go if I'm here. I expect you to keep your word," I announced as loudly as I could, noting the stone-cold faces of the armed men relaxing around the deck between Jett's and my positions.

"We did promise that," my escort from the boat confirmed, circling around in front of me with an ugly smile on his face. "But seeing as you came along so nicely, we'll give you a choice."

I was momentarily distracted from the looming threat as my cell began to buzz once more.

Backing away instinctively, I couldn't suppress a yelp as he pulled me forward and shoved his hand into my ass pocket to retrieve the still buzzing device. Four... Five... The device fell silent, and Jett roared, redoubling his efforts as the creep in front of me took his time removing his hand from my ass.

Breaking away from him, I scowled and tried to move a little closer to where Jett sat, my mind churning over how to get him out of this situation safely.

With a disinterested grunt, the man sent my cell flying into the water and refocused on me.

"As I was saying. You have a choice. Your man can go the same way as your cell phone, or he can stay with you."

My scalp tingled, the blood leaving my head as I looked out over the expanse of water and considered his chances of making it back to land. He was bleeding. Were there sharks out here? Duh, it was the ocean. But he was Jett. Hadn't he grown up on the ocean? I remembered him talking about his surfing competitions with Felix growing up.

"I'm not going anywhere," Jett growled, sitting back in a pose that looked less like giving up and more like gathering energy for his next attack.

"Jett," I started, but his sharp look shut me up. There wasn't a good option for him, and it seemed cruel to make a decision he didn't want.

"Okay," I said, maintaining eye contact with him as I spoke.

"Excellent. Now, your parents have requested you leave a final message on your vlog. Kind of a party girl having fun moments before her death kind of thing," the guy who seemed to be in charge of things announced.

Jett's face dropped in a mask of shock, and it occurred to me just how much he'd missed in the few short hours since he had been taken.

"So you already knew. Or at least suspected. Interesting."

I couldn't have cared less how interesting he found it. I had to find a way to free Jett and get us out of there. A feat that became more complicated as one of the armed bystanders led me to my own deck fixture and cuffed me in place with cable ties.

"Stay here until showtime," he muttered with a sly grin before resuming his post.

The sun was warm on my face as I sat and pondered our situation. The cable ties were tight on my wrists, and even though I had watched a ton of vlogs on escaping from hostage situations, I found the reality a much harder scenario. I couldn't reach my shoes, and even if I could, they didn't have laces on them. Jett was disappointingly barefoot as well. I didn't think the break move I'd seen people use on tape would work either.

Maybe when they filmed my final vlog, the opportunity would present itself.

I balked as the line of thinking came to an end. The thoughts beyond it were nothing but unfathomable grief at the confirmation that my own parents had decided I was worth more to them dead than alive. I'd always known they were bad people, but I never thought...

Cutting the thought off before I spiraled, I sent a silent prayer out that Sullivan's mom and sister had been safely evacuated. So much grief had been caused because of the actions of the selfish few. Would it have been better if I had never met my guys? Maybe. Certainly for Sullivan. So maybe I was among those selfish people, because despite where I found myself—along with Jett, who had faithfully remained by my side since the moment we met on the airplane—I couldn't regret a moment of the time I had spent getting to know my guys.

"Rowen," Jett muttered, leaning toward me, trying to find a semblance of privacy for us. "If you get the chance when they're filming, I want you to run. Get in that boat and don't look back, do you hear me? I want you gone."

"No." I couldn't leave him with my mess. I wouldn't.

"Rowen—"

"No. I can't. So don't ask me to. I love you. I'm not leaving."

Jett reared back as far as his restraints would allow. "You love me?" he asked. His voice had a new softness to it I'd never heard before, a vulnerability that gave me hope he still felt the same way.

"Of course I do. I love you, Jett. I should have told you the first time you said it to me in that hotel room because I felt it then, too. I'm glad Kylie was a selfish bitch, and I'm glad we had this adventure together. I just wish it didn't have to end this way."

Jett snorted and glanced around at the witnesses to my little declaration. "I don't regret a second of it. Any of it, do you hear me? No regrets. I'm glad we've got that sorted, because from now on, it's about survival. Your survival."

"Jett—"

"Do you honestly think the others would let me live if I made it back without you? Face it, sunshine, I'm with you for the long haul. Your fate is mine, so let's try to improve our odds, yeah?"

I nodded, but added defiantly, "Zephyr's the sunshine one."

"No, babe, you are. We're all caught in your orbit and are better for it. You give us the warmth and light we were all missing before. Why else would three grown men walk out on their lives without a backward glance?"

***

"All right, it's showtime," our captor announced, returning to the deck sometime later. The sun was right overhead, so I guessed it was somewhere near midday. Jett glowered at everyone who came near me, and I could have sworn I heard him growl when I was pulled to my feet and positioned in the middle of the deck with my back to the water. One of the guards pointed his rifle at Jett's kneecap.

"You're going to smile, look in the camera, and give a normal update. You're going to tell your followers how much fun you're having and that you can't wait to go to your parents' charity event on the weekend. Then you're going to sign off and sit back down in your corner. If anything other than that happens, your boyfriend is going to be missing the lower part of his leg. Understand?"

Seeing as it was impossible to misinterpret, I settled for my own glower as he forced me to sign into my account and prepared to film.

"I'm going to count down from three. Your video can be you all smiles, or gunshots. Up to you. Three, two..."

As he counted one, I forced a smile onto my face and did what I did best. Performed.

"Hi, bestie babes! It's Living Chic. I know I've been off the airwaves for a while, but I've had an amazing time on this international adventure. This will be the last post for the series because I'm heading back stateside!! You'll see me at the Never Alone charity ball this Saturday! So, for the final time, guess where I am! This little island landed on the map for celebrity lovers worldwide in twenty nineteen when its cute little locals were snapped with Thor himself! Leave your guesses in the comments, and make sure you like and follow for more content. Until next time, you only live once, so live... chic." I stumbled over the last word as the implications of my sign-off hit me, but no one seemed to notice as I was dragged back to my seat and re-secured to the deck.

"Right, lads," my cameraman said as he finished posting my vlog. "Where are we with preparations?"

"Good to go," a dark-haired man said, dumping a jerry can on the deck beside me. The smell of gas wafted out of the empty drum, reminding me nauseatingly of the night before. One by one, the guards filed off the deck and piled into the motorboat until the leader, Jett, and I were the only ones left onboard.

"In case you're hoping you could pull off another escape, be assured you can't. If you don't burn, you'll be eaten by a shark before you hit land. Enjoy." He turned, cackling, and disappeared onto the boat with the rest. A moment later, a motor whirred to life, growing louder as it passed down the near side, before fading into the distance. I looked across at Jett, who was eerily still.

"Maybe they forgot to set—"

The explosion that rocked the catamaran beneath us cut off my sentence in the most frightening way imaginable. In the aftermath, the boat listed heavily to the left.

"We're taking on water," Jett grumbled, looking around with an attitude that seemed far too cool for the situation.

"Jett, I don't want to get eaten by sharks," I confessed, trying to mirror his state of calm.

"We're not getting eaten by sharks. We just need to make sure we don't burn to death or drown. We need to get ourselves free."

I nodded, fully in support of the not burning or drowning.

"If only we had shoelaces," I muttered, disappointed with my choice of footwear.

"I don't know why you're muttering about shoes, but we need to keep calm and think. I don't know about you, but my ass is starting to burn."

Once he mentioned it, I did notice that the place where I was sitting was becoming increasingly uncomfortable. The catamaran lurched again, and I found the angle was enough that I hung from the cable ties behind my back in a way that made my shoulders strain uncomfortably.

"Jett," I said, unsure how much longer I could pretend not to panic.

"I'm thinking."

CHAPTER TWENTY FOUR

Jett

WE WERE FUCKED.

The cable ties were no longer so much around my wrists as they were in them. There were no sharp surfaces I could use to grind the plastic against to break it with friction, and on top of all that, Rowen was panicking. My girl tried hard to hide it, to be strong and fight to the end, but she was staring down death for the second time in twelve hours, and her parents were the reason for all of it.

God, I wanted nothing more than to pull her into my arms and promise her it would be all right. But seeing as I didn't have use of my arms, and that was most definitely a lie, I kept my mouth shut. The boat lurched a third time, and I winced, the cable ties taking the brunt of my bodyweight as I slipped away from the wall.

Bulkhead, I corrected, remembering my Navy friends telling me that walls were called bulkheads on ships. And toilets were called heads for some strange reason. Shit, looked like I wasn't doing as well as I thought if I was reminding myself of naval terms while we slowly sank on a burning ship. Fun times.

A faint noise on the wind brought my head up at the same time Rowen looked out over the water. A boat, nicer looking than the one that had left us to die, was streaming over the water, its wake expanding behind it like the train on a bride's dress. Three figures stood around the wheel of the vessel, one with black hair, flying in the wind, one with dark skin, and steering the vessel was a giant redhead who was hollering and waving with an urgency I secretly shared.

"How?" Rowen breathed, staring with disbelieving eyes, as though convinced they were a mirage that would disappear at any moment.

"We will always find you. You're ours," I said with a shrug.

By the look on Sullivan's face as they pulled in and carefully worked their way over to us, I was going to catch hell from the guys for endangering our girl.

I couldn't wait.

Linden produced a knife and cut us free of our bindings before the guys all rushed to start berating Rowen for leaving them without a word.

"As much as I agree with you, this can wait until we're not standing on a burning, sinking ship," I muttered, steering Rowen by the elbow toward their boat. She moved willingly with me, but spun before boarding, throwing her hands around my neck.

"I love you, Jett." Her kiss supported everything she said and so much more. It promised the future I had always wanted and told me I never had to worry about being left alone again.

"I love you, Rowen. Now get your ass on that boat."

Her laugh curled around me and warmed me more than the summer breeze that blew off the water as we left the sinking vessel behind.

Rather than pulling into Fremantle, we headed down the coast, beaching the boat in Rockingham, where the others informed me they'd fled after the fire.

"We'll go back for the van later," Sullivan assured us, slapping me on the back in a friendly check-in that I appreciated. Of all the guys, I had gotten to know him best, and despite how things started, I knew he was reliable and an all-around stand-up dude.

"But how did you find us?" Rowen blurted as we sat on the seawall and looked out over the ocean we'd just narrowly escaped.

"Makenna. How else?" Sullivan grunted.

"Care to elaborate?" I asked, knowing he was being short because he was hurt about her running off on them.

Sullivan sighed and turned to face Rowen. "She called your cell to tell you about a press release draft she found in that file she's been looking into. It was announcing your death and the tragedy that it happened so close to their charity bullshit."

"I don't think it said *bullshit*," Rowen admonished with a smile.

"I'm paraphrasing here. Anyway, when she couldn't get you again, she tracked your cell. Gave us our marching orders along with your coordinates. The rest is history. You have a solid friend there, but maybe don't piss her off."

Rowen laughed again, then took Sullivan's hand. "I'm sorry I left. If I thought I had any other choice, I wouldn't have done it. But we were talking about Jett's life. I don't care what any of you say, I can't live without all of you, so don't make me regret doing for him—doing for any of you—what you would do for me. I love you. All four of you."

Sullivan's brow relaxed the longer she spoke, and by the time she was professing her love, he was putty in her hand. The big bad bounty hunter was a simp for our girl.

***

Perth airport was relatively quiet compared to some of the other airports we had been in as we made our way through check in and security.

As we wrapped up our reunion chat on the beach, Makenna called Sullivan's cell and demanded to be put on speaker. After congratulating Rowen and me on our deaths, she advised that she had organized fake IDs and passports to be dropped to us along with tickets to Fiji. All we had to do was meet her contact at the airport and get on the flight.

Zephyr had lost his mind, trauma forgotten, at the idea of surfing the Fijian breaks and finally settling down somewhere. Makenna had promised she was working on purchasing a house for us and would have details before we landed. Sullivan was right. She was scary.

As Zephyr steered everyone toward the food court, espousing the virtues of a full stomach, I eyed the restrooms and, more specifically, the shower room.

Slipping my hand in Rowen's, I urged her to a stop before whispering, "Come with me."

Her giggle sent electricity racing straight to my balls, and I shot a quick look at Sullivan, waiting for his nod before pulling her into the cubicle and locking us in.

"I'm starting to think showers are our thing," Rowen muttered, her hands pushing beneath my shirt as she pressed the length of her body along mine.

"I'm fine with that," I said, gathering her hair in a fist and tugging her head back for a punishing kiss.

She moaned into my mouth, her busy hands working my belt and pants, but as she made to sink to her knees, I tightened my grip and steered her toward the dressing mirror mounted on the back of the door.

"We don't know how dirty this room is, and you deserve better than to be on your knees in a public restroom. Besides, I'd rather see you with your hands smudging this mirror, watching me take you hard from behind. You scared the hell out of me today, and I have to admit, I want to punish you a little." I stepped out of my pants, fishing for my wallet, when Rowen's hand covered my own.

"I want you bare. We can sort out birth control later, but I want to feel you. To know you're really here. Is that all right?"

I had never gone bare with anyone, but the idea of filling her up made a primal part of me sit up and take notice.

"Hands on the mirror," I growled, reaching around her hips and pulling her shorts and panties to her knees. Kicking her feet wider, I pressed on the small of her back until she was nicely stretched out.

"You're soaked for me," I said, running two fingers up and down her slit, admiring how they glistened in the artificial lighting.

"You know I love you, right?" I asked lightly, extending my exploration up to her ass crack and back down.

"Yes," she replied without hesitation.

"Good, because I'm about to fuck you like I don't."

Positioning my cock at her entrance, I thrust into her on one hard stroke, setting a punishing pace that made her hands slip around on the reflective surface in front of us. All the stress of the previous twenty-four hours, all the insecurities I had about sharing her with three other men, left me as I pounded into her until hers weren't the only legs shaking under the strain.

Shifting my hands on her hips, I ran one thumb down to her ass and circled gently around her hole.

"Yes," she hissed, tilting her hips slightly higher.

I grinned and pressed in as a heavy breath escaped her. She was everything to me. Everything. And with new identities, and a new country to see, I finally felt like I'd come home for the first time in my life. I wouldn't be a soldier in this new iteration of self, but maybe I could be something more.

Rowen shifted, taking her weight on one hand and reaching down to rub furiously at her clit, chasing the precipice I was already balancing on. Her body tightened, trapping my thumb and squeezing my cock so that I had no choice but to follow her over the edge as she screamed through her climax.

Pulling out of her slowly, I watched in satisfaction as my cum slid out onto her leg. Following a possessive instinct I didn't fully understand, I scooped it up with two fingers, pressing it back inside her as she shivered through aftershocks.

Dressing quickly, I waited until her breathing had slowed, then pulled her shorts and panties back into place and winked at her.

"I want you to spend the day knowing I'm inside you."

Before she could reply, I unlocked the door and waved her ahead of me with a gallant arm.

Pecking a kiss on my cheek, she skipped past me and over to a table where the others sat with trays full of food waiting to be consumed.

Sullivan glanced at his watch meaningfully as I approached the table. "That didn't take long. Maybe you need to join in on group activities, or read Zephyr's notes for some tips."

I flipped him the bird as I stole his cola and pulled our girl onto my lap.

New life, new country, new family, I thought again.

I couldn't wait.

"Oh, shit," Zephyr cursed, nose buried in his cell. "Rowen, you need to see this."

Still reeling from Zephyr using an actual curse word, I snatched the cell he shoved in our girl's face and placed it face up on the table. A live NBC stream showed a distinguished couple being led from their house in handcuffs. I cranked the volume on the device and leaned closer, but could only hear snatches of the news anchor reporting on the couple's 'conspiracy to murder' and 'attempt to defraud'.

Rowen sat so still I wondered if she was breathing. Tightening my arm around her waist, I tugged until she relaxed against me. "That's them, isn't it?" I asked quietly enough that no one beyond our table would hear.

"Yeah," She said. "That's my parents."

"Makenna sent me the link," Zephyr said, watching her closely. It was one thing to know something, but another to see the consequences playing out.

The movement started as a small tremor, escalating in seconds to a full body shake as Rowen threw her head back and laughed. The four of us watched as our girl went to the point of hysteria before taking a deep breath and grinning at us one at a time.

"We're free."

EPILOGUE

Rowen

AFTER A TEN-HOUR FLIGHT, WE LANDED IN NADI TO find a driver waiting for us at the arrivals gate. I wondered if Mak had ever considered being a travel agent. *Probably too legal, and not enough fun*, I decided as we piled into a beat-up truck and headed out. With my men all around me chatting and making plans for the next few days, I couldn't say how long we drove for, but eventually we pulled up to a gated property close to the sea-shore. Zephyr whooped at the sight of the waves breaking over the sand, and I gaped at the beautiful two-story house that came into view.

Gravel crunched under the truck's tires as we pulled up to the top of the drive, and as we piled out and started retrieving our baggage, we found another surprise. The front door flew open with a bang, and a streak of red hair flew down the stairs and launched itself at Sullivan.

"Sully!"

For his part, Sullivan caught the little girl out of instinct, his face a mask of shock.

"Ray. What are you doing here?"

Rather than answering him, the ball of energy turned toward me and let out a deafening shriek.

"Oh em gee! Living Chic!"

"You can call me Rowen," I said, flushing at the look of worship in her eyes that perfectly mirrored the blue of her older brother.

"Rowen. Oh my Jesus. Come in! I'll put the kettle on. Do you drink tea?"

"Ray," Sullivan tried again.

"There's a free room next to mine you can take. It's really pretty. Can we be friends? It's going to be so fun living together. Are you excited?"

Rayleigh's questions continued as we made our way inside and discovered the interior of the house was cozy and lived in.

"I suppose we can always renovate," Linden murmured, scrunching his nose at the seventies era floral wallpaper that lined the foyer.

"I like it. It's... homey," I said, moving into the kitchen space and leaving Sullivan to try to explain to his sister why I would be sleeping at the other end of the house.

I grinned to myself, wandering from room to room and imagining the life we could build here, away from my parents and public attention, away from obligation and killers that I wasn't in love with. Perfection.

"You should be in bed now, anyway. It's late, Ray," Sullivan announced. "There'll be plenty of time in the morning to get to know everyone. We can even see about getting you into a school. No more home-schooling."

Rayleigh scowled, and it was the cutest thing. It was the exact expression I was so used to seeing on Sullivan's face but delivered by a smaller, more feminine version.

"Go sleep. I promise we'll be here in the morning. Which room is Mam in?"

Ray trotted off to show Sullivan the wing that she and her mom had settled in, while I followed the others to the opposite end of the house.

In a room that looked more like a studio apartment than a bedroom, we found two queen-sized beds pushed together facing a floor-to-ceiling sliding door. While Zephyr disappeared into the attached ensuite, I wandered out onto the balcony and felt the sea air on my face as I fished my new cell from my pocket.

Three months ago, I never imagined this would be my life. In fact, I wouldn't have had a life if it weren't for one person. Dialing the familiar number, I held the cell to my ear and counted out the rings. Surprisingly, the call connected almost immediately, and though the voice on the other end was friendly, it wasn't who I was expecting.

"Rowen! Oh my god, you made it! Thank God. How are you? Are you safe? Mak has been keeping me up to date, but I've been worried about you."

"Sloane."

"Are you sure you're okay?"

My heart warmed to hear her voice. New York felt like a different lifetime—someone else's life, really—and I had no idea what my friends had been up to since I last saw them.

"I'm fine," I said, settling onto one of the outdoor chairs. "How have you been?"

"Good. I've been good. I have an interview for a new job. You'll never guess what it is."

I laughed. "I'm out of practice guessing. Can I have a clue?"

"I'm interning on *Shifting Sands!*" Her scream was loud enough that I had to pull the cell away from my ear.

"That's amazing! You'll get it for sure. Hey, sorry to jump in, but it's super late here. Where's Mak?"

Sloane went quiet for a moment, and I felt my heart seize. Had all her extracurricular activities caught up with her? Had she been flagged for all the work she'd done to keep me safe?

I wouldn't be able to handle it if I was responsible for bringing danger to her door.

"Sloane, what's going on? Where's Mak?"

Sloane cleared her throat, as though choosing her words carefully.

"She's just dealing with a little something at the moment. I swear, it's nothing to do with your stuff. She wanted me to tell you that she ordered you a double king bed, but there's a wait on it. Oh! Also, don't be surprised if there are people there when you get to the house. She got Sullivan's mother and sister set up there as well. We're going to come visit you soon, too, so we can meet these guys and make sure they're good enough for our girl."

I grinned as Linden appeared in the doorway, a question in his eyes.

"I can't wait to see you guys. If Mak's busy, I won't bother her, but please tell her thank you. I literally owe her my life a few thousand times over, so if there's anything I can do to help, just call. I love you guys."

"Love you too, babe. Ooh, adverts are over. Got to go."

I chuckled as I terminated the call and wandered inside to join my men.

"Our first night in a bed big enough for all of us. Dibs on the middle," Zephyr announced, launching himself onto the mattress.

Linden moved in behind me and ran his hands from my shoulders to my wrists, then leaned in and pressed a chaste kiss to the skin under my ear.

"A perfect time to christen the bed, unless you're tired, love."

"Not at all," I said, tossing my cell on the bedside table and stripping my shirt off.

Sullivan appeared in the doorway and leaned against the jamb, taking in the sight of me shirtless with Linden behind me and Zephyr on the bed.

"In or out?" Jett groused, coming up behind him.

"I could ask you the same thing, mate," Sullivan retorted. Both men moved into the room and secured the door.

This was a turning point. Jett had avoided a lot of the group activities, preferring to have me to himself in the moments we could snatch alone. One by one, he met the eyes of each of the men in the room before moving that lovely forest-green gaze to me last. I opened my mouth, ready to make excuses for him. To defuse the tension of the moment and assure everyone that I was fine as things stood.

"In," he said decisively, whipping his shirt off without breaking eye contact and moving toward the bed.

"Always in."

Thank you so much for reading Where in the World. If you enjoyed getting to know Rowen and her guys, please consider leaving a review here

---

Want to know more about Makenna the candy-loving computer wiz? She will be starring in her very own series, The one for us which starts with The not so secret life of a wish maker. Preorder Today!

Sign up for TL's newsletter to find out about new books!

Turn the page for a sneak peek of The Not So Secret Life of a Wish Maker...

THE NOT SO SECRET LIFE OF A WISH MAKER

(One year before Rowen received her email)

Prologue

Makenna

"You're hot, but you are such an asshole," I growled, staring down Zaxton's stupid smirk from far too small a distance.

"Yup," he agreed, unrepentant.

A crash from downstairs, followed by the titter of laughter, reminded me why this was a stupid idea. We were here to celebrate Christmas in July, dammit. My brothers, my best friends, my freaking parents, were all downstairs preparing a feast and hanging out while I'd snuck off with this idiot.

"You don't deserve all this. I should just leave you here and go back downstairs."

"That would be a lot more convincing if you didn't have your hand on my dick."

Huh. I did too. The ridge beneath my palm was long and thick in a way that would have made me shiver, except that I knew better than to show weakness in front of this jerk.

Instead, I squeezed tighter and frowned. "That's a little disappointing."

Zaxton's jaw dropped before he caught himself, teeth coming together with an audible click. "How about you put that mouth to good use for me?" he suggested, running a hand up into my hair. Knocking his hand away, I shook my head. "How about you use yours instead?"

"Ok."

The next moment, a shove sent me sprawling across my childhood bed. Pillows and teddy bears crashed into the hideous salmon-pink wall behind my bed, and I gave a silent apology to my tattered Wile E. Coyote doll as I pushed him off after the rest. His innocent eyes did not need to see what was about to happen here.

"This is only happening once. Never again. And no one needs to know about it. Deal?" I panted as he pushed my Santa's elf dress up over my hips and pulled at the waistband of my panties.

"You think I want to be known as the guy who fucked his best friend's little sister?"

"Shut up. And it's only happening now because I'm bored and horny," I said.

Zaxton reached a hand up and covered my mouth. Something hard bumped against my teeth. Chocolate.

The bastard was using my weakness against...

As the sugary treat melted on my tongue, blanketing my tastebuds in the familiar comfort of Hershey's best, Zaxton slid his arms beneath my knees and dove face-first into my pussy. God... damn. This wasn't fair. My brain flooded with dopamine, my senses overwhelmed by the combination of chocolate and Zaxton's talented tongue, assisted by the silver barbell that had inspired this stupid venture in the first place.

Turns out tongue piercings were a gift from the orgasm gods.

Grabbing Zaxton's curly brown head with one hand, and a fluffy pink throw pillow with the other, I slammed the latter over my face to smother the scream that tore out of my throat. Squeezing Zax's ears with my thighs, I kept him in place as I rode the waves of my release. Partly because I wasn't ready to be finished, but mostly so I didn't have to see the satisfied look I knew would be on his smug face.

"That's one," he muttered.

"What...?"

"Gotta be five, right?"

Bastard. I may have had a small, barely noticeable preference for the number five. Of course he was going to use it against... My breath caught as he went back to work and pushed me straight over the edge once again.

Damn, this was getting embarrassing. As he surged over me, his grin as wide and triumphant as I knew it would be, I decided it would have been far healthier to find another outlet for my quarter life crisis. I could have bought a new computer. Hacked NASA and taken the *Perseverance* on a tour of Mars. Stolen scripts for the next season of *Shifting Sands* for Sloane—not that she'd have appreciated it. Her moral compass was way less skewed than my own. Or, I could have chosen someone who wasn't my mortal enemy to work out the stress of being forced to move back into my parents' house. Apparently, MIT didn't take kindly to students accepting hypothetical challenges from teachers and crashing every server on campus. I thought they were more sore about the fact they needed me to restart the system because none of the teachers could overwrite my code. Potato, potahto. It all led to the same conclusion. Me living back in this pink nightmare of a room with no clue what to do with my life.

So I decided to screw Zaxton, the ass.

"Roll over," he said, slapping my thigh as he worked his button fly one handed.

"Forget it. You can look me in the eye while I fuck you," I snapped, snatching away the condom he pulled from his discarded pants and ripping it open with my teeth.

"Only one of us is in charge here, Princess, and it ain't you."

I rolled my eyes and offered him the prophylactic, ignoring how he took his time covering himself up. I hadn't lied; the asshat was seriously attractive. If you didn't have to tolerate his personality. He prowled over me once more, corded forearms coming to rest on either side of my head.

"You ready?" he asked, uncharacteristic concern on his face.

Nope. We weren't doing that.

In a coordinated move I couldn't repeat if I tried, I flipped our positions and sank onto his erection with a groan.

Keeping one hand on his crazy-hard stomach, I set my pace, grinding on him in a way that sent my over-sensitized flesh into tingles of delight.

"Having fun?" Zaxton asked, resting his hands behind his head as his eyes traveled over me.

"Shut up. You're ruining the fantasy that you're just a really good dildo," I panted, my thighs trembling with the beginnings of a third orgasm.

As logical thought left me, the world went on a tilt a whirl and I found myself beneath a scowling Zaxton as he took over the pace, pushing me through the third and into a toe curling fourth orgasm.

Shit. This was intense.

He pounded into me, shaking the frame of my twin bed in a dangerously loud symphony of squeaks that i hoped would be absorbed by the volume of the crowd below. His body seized a moment later, teeth sinking into my collarbone in a vicious bite as he groaned through his own release.

As soon as his trembling frame stilled, he pulled away, dressing efficiently as my sex addled brain struggled to catch up.

"Wait... that was..."

"Only four. I know." He threw me a wink and sidled out of my room a moment later.

"Son of a bitch!" I hurled the nearest teddy bear at hand at the closing door and grumbled through a fifth 'self serve' orgasm before righting myself and heading downstairs.

In the kitchen, I ran into one of my best friends, Rowen, who took one look at me and froze. The glass she had been filling with water overflowed before she caught herself and moved toward the sink.

"So..." she started, eyeing me.

"I decided to make the third bad thing happen before it happened to me. Kicked out of school, moving into my parents' place, slept with my mortal enemy. There's the trifecta. Now fate can leave me alone."

"That's not really healthy, you know."

"Save me the lecture please, Living Chic, I just want my bestie right now."

Rowen slummed it with Sloane and me a lot, but she came from high society and had a successful vlog as her online persona, Living Chic. She had recently wrapped up a killer series on hackers with help from yours truly. Even though her parents were the worst kind of people, Rowen was the best, and I loved her like the sister I always wanted. That didn't mean I needed to hear her opinions on my well-founded superstitions.

"Where's Sloane?" I asked, trying to change the subject. Rowen raised her eyebrow and glanced pointedly at the living room door. Watching *Shifting Sands*. I should have known. Our other best friend was arguably the quirkiest of our friends group. Her obsession with the melodramatic daytime soap was unparalleled, and something that would make a therapist very rich someday. But she was the kindest, most considerate best friend anyone could ever ask for. Fishing a bag of Hershey's kisses from the back of the pantry, I nodded to the back lawn where mom had set up a series of picnic tables long enough to seat our family and friends.

"Shall we?"

Rowen mopped up her spilled water and followed me outside. As we made our way to the opposite end of the rapidly filling table, I unwrapped two kisses and popped them in my mouth. Claiming the seat beside Wolf, one of my brother's roommates, I offered him a fist bump and settled back as tray after tray of food passed down the table.

Out of nowhere, a small hand snatched my bag of kisses away. "No candy until after lunch. You're a grown ass woman, Makenna, you shouldn't be eating this trash, anyway."

"Mom!" I protested, casting a forlorn look at the bag as it disappeared into her apron pocket. Without a backward glance she made her way to the other end of the table. I huffed a frustrated breath, slumped in my chair and passed on the next few dishes until a brown-wrapped bar of goodness appeared on my plate.

"You're the best, Wolf," I whispered, squirreling the contraband beneath the table before anyone could notice. From the corner of my eye, I saw Wolf lift a shoulder as he continued to serve himself potato salad, but a slight smirk lit his face.

"Can I get everyone's attention for a minute?" Mom called from the head of the table. Sloane wandered out of the house and crept down the line of the table to slide into the empty seat beside Rowen. "Glad you could join us, dear," Mom said. Sloane ducked her head, avoiding everyone's eyes as Mom continued. "Welcome to Christmas in July,

Fairburn style. We'll be exchanging gifts after we eat, but first I wanted to thank everyone for attending today and acknowledge the other big news we have. Jared, my baby boy, has finally proposed to Cindy! And they're buying a house. Congratulations, you two." Applause briefly flared around the table and I felt my cheeks burn. All five of my brothers were married or engaged. Working in successful jobs and doing the family name proud. By comparison, I was a college dropout who bent the limits of the law and was about to be stuck living back under our parents' roof. Unwrapping the Hershey's bar with hands that shook, I shoved a large piece in my mouth and tried to tune out anything that wasn't the sweet taste on my tongue as Jared stood up to make a speech.

"... I know I left you guys in the lurch, moving out so suddenly, but Asher and I were talking and we think we've come up with a plan that could work for everyone. Makenna can take my room in the apartment." The sound of my name hauled me back to the here and now, and mentally rewinding the speech, I realized my lovely brother may have helped solve one of my problems. Living with a bunch of guys I'd known for years trumped moving back in with my parents any day of the week and twice on Sundays. I glanced at Wolf, who squeezed my knee in support, then at Riaz, who winked. Riaz was the consummate flirt, so I expected nothing less from him. Avoiding Zaxton's hard glare, I looked at the only person who mattered in this situation. Asher owned the mortgage to the apartment and all the liability that went along with it. Clearly, he'd had more than one conversation with Jared about this because there was nothing but approval on his face. I wondered what his girlfriend, Sharnie, would think, then decided I didn't care.

"I'm in," I said, grinning and hoping this wasn't the worst idea ever.

Preorder The not so secret life of a wish maker today!

ALSO BY TL HAMILTON

M/F Sports Romance

The Perfect Stroke

Split - Kane & Darcy Pt 1

Shatter - Kane & Darcy Pt 2

Shock - Evie & Xavier

Contemporary RH

The One For Us

The not so secret life of a wish maker

The not so secret life of a candy addict (coming soon)

Where in the world (Stand alone in 'The One For Us' universe)

Paranormal RH

Moon Dust Library/ Silver Springs Library Standalones

Moonlit Alexandrite

Moonlit Alexandrite: Crafty Seductions

Jewels Cafe: Jacinth

ABOUT THE AUTHOR

TL Hamilton hails from Melbourne, Australia, where she lives with her hubby, two little boys, Arlo the wonder pup, and Hugo the turtle.

The consummate daydreamer, TL writes all over the romance spectrum from romcom right through to the dark, gritty hold onto your seats drama. Regardless of the story, you can guarantee you'll find relatable characters and steamy bedroom times between the covers of her books.

Reviews are the life blood of indie authors, so if you read her work and enjoy it, please consider leaving a review in exchange for her everlasting adoration.

ACKNOWLEDGMENTS

If you've made it this far, my first acknowledgment is to you, the reader.

Thank you so much for coming on another fictional journey with me. Your support is what lets me continue creating these characters I love so much (and I hope you do too!)

To my advanced reader team, thank you again for taking the time to give feedback and spread the word on my latest vivid daydream. A special mention must go to Jamie, my amazing alpha reader who is always the first to see the messy accumulation of ideas that is my first draft.

Katie and Zainab, you two are the best. You both have an amazing way of taking my words and polishing them until they gleam and I appreciate you both for being there, even when the words take their sweet time to come.

To my family and friends, who patiently listen to every new idea and crazy concept I announce and encourage me to keep going when the writing isn't as easy, thank you. I couldn't do this without your support.

Special mention to my author friends, you know who you are, you guys are amazing and between animal memes, GIF conversations, and empathy over muse issues, it isn't an exaggeration to say this book wouldn't have happened without your support.

A huge thank you to River and Kismet New Moon designs for my stunning cover, and a final thank you to Sarah, my PA for your help in promoting this book.

I hope I'll see you all next book and until then, happy reading!